The First Time

The First Time

Women Speak Out About "Losing Their Virginity"

Karen Bouris

Afterword by Louanne Cole, Ph.D., Sexology

Conari Press
Berkeley, CA

Copyright ©1993 by Karen Bouris; afterword ©1993 by Louanne Cole, Ph.D.

All Rights Reserved. No part of this book may be used or reproduced in any manner whatsoever without written permission, except in the case of brief quotations in critical articles or reviews. For information, contact Conari Press, 1144 65th St., Suite B, Emeryville, CA 94608.

Printed in the United States of America on recycled paper

Cover Design: Sharon Smith
Cover Illustration: Auguste Rodin, *Clothed Woman Sitting in Three-Quarter Profile with a Hand on Her Shoulder*. (D. 4748), Musee Rodin, Paris. Photograph: Bruno Jarret

Excerpts from *Erotic Wars* by Lillian Rubin. Copyright ©1990 by Lillian Rubin. Reprinted by permission of Farrar, Straus & Giroux, Inc.

Library of Congress Cataloging-in-Publication Data
Bouris, Karen, 1968-
        The first time : women speak out about "losing their virginity" /
Karen Bouris : afterword by Louanne Cole.
            p.   cm.
        ISBN 0-943233-50-X : $18.95
        1. Women—United States—Sexual Behavior   2. Defloration
        3. Women—United States—Interviews.   I. Title.
HQ29.B69 1993   93-5805
306.7'082--dc20   CIP

*For
the women who shared their stories,
and for those who read them with an open heart*

Acknowledgements

Thanks to Conari Press, for not only giving me the opportunity to write, but believing that I could do it. And especially to MJ, the player of so many roles—from mentor to editor—who patiently held my hand, guiding me, and who continues to do so in infinite ways.

I want to thank the following people I used as resources: Marsha McCoy at the University of Kansas, the East Bay NOW chapter, Roger and Cindy at CAL-PEP, the multitude of anonymous women's shelters and clinics, the members of the Wild Women Association, and the many other people who shared their time, energy, and resources with me.

Thanks to my parents. My mother fed me healthy food while I paced and procrastinated. Growing up, my father told me I could achieve anything I wanted if I put my mind to it. Thanks also to my best friend and sister of my heart, Jackie, to Erin and Stacy, providers of pep talks and fajitas, to Scott and Pal, my steady supporters, and to sweet Simon, who always gave me himself to look forward to.

Contents

The First Time

"How deep the need is to tell the story, to hear it to the end."

—*Susan Griffin,*
A Chorus of Stones

We know ourselves by the stories we tell. Each person is like a tree, with layers marking growth, each having weathered a different year of storms and sun, warm breezes and shaded silences. And like the rings that tell the story of the tree's life, our growth is revealed by stories, by the words we tell ourselves and others about our experiences. We find communion by sharing our stories and discovering similar threads of experience.

One of the most significant stories a woman can tell is the experience of her first sexual intercourse. Not only is the event a traditional rite of passage into womanhood, but it is the door to one of the most intriguing and sacred sides of herself—her sexuality. Unfortunately, for many women the first time they have intercourse isn't by choice; prey to miseducation, abuse, coercion, or outright violence, they have the decision taken from them. For others, however, it is the beginning of sexual discovery and romance, independence and physical communication; it may even be the first adult decision they feel they make.

No matter what the experience—joyful or scarring, meaningful or seemingly irrelevant—it can mark the threshold of the expression of our physical relationship with others. The stories we hold and the stories we tell of this time are important to us as individuals—and as women trying to make sense of the mysterious and intriguing experience of sex.

I remember looking through the shelves of women's books in bookstores a couple years ago. There were books on tantric loving, on masturbation, on improving both heterosexual and homosexual technique. A wave of erotic literature had hit the shelves, along with several landmark studies about female sexuality. But *nothing* on virginity loss except a few statistics on age of sexual initiation. With all of the studies and books talking about practicalities—what is a clitoris, how many times a week do women masturbate, does anyone ever have orgasms from intercourse—and the erotic, the emotional experience seemed to be almost completely ignored.

I found it odd in all that research, all that exploration of female sexuality, nobody ever asked the questions: What was your sexual initiation like? How did you feel about "losing your virginity"? Why hadn't anybody dealt with the subject? Was it an unspoken taboo, considered boring, inconsequential, tragic? We know so much about the mechanics of sex, about women's sexual fantasies, even the most popular time of year to lose your virginity (summer), but we have neglected the engaged heart and body—and the passage that leads to or tears us away from this.

Granted, it is difficult to study psychological and emotional experience. The range of variables, as with any psychological survey, are tremendous. But I wanted to know what other women felt about their "first time," and what impact it had had on their future sexuality. So I decided to find out myself.

I began by drafting a questionnaire, testing it out on friends, and revising it until I felt that it was impartial yet specific enough to get honest answers to my questions. My main goal was to create a safe space for women to share the intimate details of their stories no matter what the experience. I wanted to provide a forum for women to express themselves, a way to talk about not only the event itself, but how they felt about it and how they viewed the experience in light of later ones. I decided to ask open-ended questions, which I hoped would lead each woman to an exploration of the emotional aspect of her sexuality, a chance to see patterns and turning points, beginning with sexual initiation.

One thousand questionnaires went out to such women's organizations as shelters, support groups, and professional associations, to clubs, colleges, and special-interest-group mailing lists, and to friends and professional contacts; I also interviewed women who felt more comfortable speaking than writing, from homeless women to busy working mothers.

Over 150 women from all walks of life—teachers and

students, psychologists and writers, waitresses and security guards, lawyers and ministers, prostitutes and
sorority members—answered the questionnaire. An entire human sexuality class from a University responded.
The average (median, mean, *and* mode) age of first
intercourse was seventeen. Although I tried to get as
broad a racial mix of women as possible, the overwhelming majority of respondents were white—85 percent to be exact—whereas 9 percent were African American, 3 percent Hispanic, and 3 percent Asian. I tried
specifically to reach minority women through a variety
of organizations, clubs, and personal contacts, but so-
cial/ethnic taboos about discussing sexuality might
have discouraged some women from answering, as
well as the fact that I am a white, middle-class woman.
Most religious upbringings were represented, including Protestant, Baptist, Presbyterian, Methodist, Jewish, and Catholic.

Geographically, the largest number of respondents
were from California, making up 20 percent of the total.
Regionally, 30 percent came from the West, 39 percent
from the Midwest, 6 percent from the Southeast, and 23
percent from the Northeast; 2 percent from outside the
U.S. Approximately 10 percent of the respondents defined themselves as lesbians; about 25 percent had had
a sexual experience with a woman.

The lack of response from older women was particularly noticeable. The age range ran from thirteen to
seventy-four, but the average age was thirty-three. It's

not hard to imagine that for older women, who grew up in a very different social climate, the mere inquiry was an invasion. A few wrote to tell me so. One seventy-five-year-old white Presbyterian said, "Thank you for the questionnaire, but I shall have to let you down. My friends and I were raised in a far different era—with different standards and a different moral code. There were no therapists or self-help groups. If we had any problems, we 'shed a few tears,' 'thought we would die,' and in a few days were back to normal. Sounds simple, I know. So to fill out your questionnaire just isn't part of our world. I hope you understand."

"I have to just keep telling myself that these are changing times," writes a seventy-six-year-old black woman from South Carolina. "My granddaughters try to keep me up on things, but sometimes, I cannot believe how things have changed. The things they do, the things they talk about! I am trying to keep up and accept the differences. But I'd like to keep my own story and bedroom goings-on to myself."

A sixty-seven-year-old white Catholic from Massachusetts echoes this sentiment. "There are some things in life which I feel should be your very own. Also, because of my very early training to not unburden myself to others, I don't think I ever felt close enough to any woman to discuss such intimate details."

A few other women wrote back to say that they were refusing to fill out the questionnaire or talk to me. The reasons varied but the reactions were revealing. One eighty-year-old woman said, "It happened so long ago, has been buried so deep, that to dredge it up now would be too difficult." And a prostitute said, "I'll tell you anything but that." I also got responses questioning my intentions: "Are you a pervert? A lesbian?" or, simply, "What business is it of yours?"

The responses I did get were tremendous. Something about telling the story to a neutral party gave women the guts to look at themselves and their sexuality, often with startling insight. Women exposed their secret, sexual self, a self usually reserved for intimate bedroom discussions or meetings with a therapist, or deemed too private to show anyone at all. Many women said, "Thank you for asking this question," and others commented that it had been therapeutic to write down their story; some confided things that they had never before told anyone.

Through the series of questions (see Appendix), women shared their disappointments: "I should have valued myself more and not 'given away' my virginity to the first guy who wanted my body but not necessarily me." They shared their anger: "Now whenever I see this man/boy who date-raped me, I want to punch him in the face, hurt him, and make him feel as ugly as he made me feel." And they shared their growth: "Finally, through making love with a caring, compassionate man, I was shown how special, unique, and attractive I was; he gave me a wonderful gift—a new image of myself." Because of the intimate nature of the questions, all of the names in the stories have been changed to insure confidentiality, and other identifying characteristics were also altered slightly, with only general references to where women were raised and religious background or occupation.

The stories I chose to include were those that I thought shared a common thread of experience but were also revealing of the individual. The passionate responses testify to the powerful emotions that women have about this experience. They offer a keyhole glimpse into the gamut of feelings, opinions, and beliefs women have about their own sexuality.

Because I asked specific questions about how first sexual experiences affected their later sexuality, many women took the opportunity to give me an overview of their sexuality. In general, the older, more experienced the woman, the more she told of the metamorphosis of her sexuality, a positive transformation that took place over the years; over and over women disclosed that the older they got, the better sex was.

Often it took women years to learn about their bodies and what they needed and wanted sexually. Some women needed to let go of stereotypes they had: how their bodies were "supposed" to function, and how women were "supposed" to act during sex. Other women needed to learn to trust their partner in order to communicate their needs. Age also often brought about a change in women's ideas about the myths of fairy-tale romance, and gave them perspective to redesign ingrained images to fit their own reality. With experience and maturity, women began to say what was important to them, to ask for what they needed, and to expect respect and support.

As I began to look at the questionnaires and interviews as a whole, I saw certain themes emerging. There were many issues surrounding the relationship between sex and power, whether feelings of empowerment, powerlessness, or using sex to have power over men. As much as power was an issue, so was choice, in all of its forms and gradations. Some women felt liberated by the choice they had consciously made. Others felt like sideline observers or passive participants in something that coincidentally happened to them—they were not aware they even had a choice. And still others had had the choice stripped from them by rape and other forms of abuse. Not surprisingly, the women who reported a positive experience almost always needed to feel love to enjoy sex; emotional connection seemed to be the gateway to physical pleasure. It also helped to have a sensitive partner.

The tremendous changes in sexual mores and behaviors over the past thirty years were clearly reflected in the differing responses between older and younger generations; not only was there a greater openness to share their experiences among younger women, but there was also less adherence to the notion of the need to preserve virginity and more claiming the right to sexual experience. The cutoff age seemed to be fifty—

women over fifty had either "saved" their virginity for their wedding night, or at least felt they were supposed to. Women in their thirties and forties, who grew up in the sexually liberated sixties and seventies, more comfortably claimed their right to premarital sex and told tales of many sexual partners, whereas young women in their twenties and teens grapple with fear of AIDS and other sexually transmitted diseases along with pressure toward early sexual initiation.

Against the backdrop of all these experiences are individual responses to a set of sexual "rules" for women, the cornerstone of which traditionally has been virginity until marriage. Taken generationally, the broad spectrum of stories represents the breakdown of the old rule, the ensuing confusion and conflicting pressures both to have and not have sex, and the discovery process which we, as a society, are in now.

Lillian Rubin, in her book *Erotic Wars,* discusses the unconscious nature of these rules. "How do we learn these sexual rules? I don't remember anyone explicitly saying those words to me. Yet I knew, as surely as I knew the time of day or the day of the week. For the sexual norms of an age are passed on to the young in a thousand unseen and unspoken ways, as much in what is never said or named as in what is."

Nowhere did women react more strongly to the existence of such norms than in their reactions to the concept of "losing your virginity," which is why I've devoted an entire chapter to responses to this question.

Largely, women were dissatisfied with the social value placed on female virginity, and were offended by sexual initiation being considered a loss. As one woman explained, "I don't feel as if we really 'lose' anything with our first sexual experience. I feel we gain a better understanding of ourselves and our bodies; knowledge about sex and sexuality; and a greater amount of self-confidence. My sexual partners have made me feel much more comfortable about my body, which overall makes me feel better about myself, so when I 'lost my virginity,' I gained a whole lot more." Some women thought that the term was appropriate, because they felt they had lost something through the experience: their youthful innocence, a private part of themselves, or a coveted bargaining chip.

Others resented the emphasis on penile-vaginal intercourse as the ultimate sexual experience. As one woman wrote, "If the idea is that a woman's a virgin until she has penile-vaginal intercourse, there is also an idea that the only sex that counts is intercourse. I beg to differ. By still using the term 'losing your virginity,' we are allowing a notion that sex equals intercourse to continue. By ignoring other sexual activities, like oral sex or manual stimulation because they are part of foreplay, we are ignoring other ways to feel pleasure and share our sexual feelings. We are also overlooking the activities in which most women (as well as men) orgasm. If we don't consider oral sex as high as intercourse on some sexual scales, most of us will feel we are weird or inadequate if we don't orgasm during intercourse but do during oral sex. It's very limited to consider that we are virgins until we are penetrated. It is just as restricting to base our sexual norms and scripts on one particular sexual activity."

The notion that the act of intercourse is the ultimate goal ignores or undermines much of our sensuality, notes sexologist Marty Klein in *Ask Me Anything.* "[We] need a broader view of sexuality. Intercourse and even orgasm are optional parts of a sexual experience. Describing everything else as 'getting ready for sex' robs us of the deep satisfaction available from kissing, caressing, teasing, and oral and manual stimulation."

Nonetheless, the hallmark of sexual initiation for most people continues to be heterosexual penile-vaginal intercourse, and what emerged from the questionnaires is that even in this day and age, we have conflicting feelings and beliefs about the first time we perform this act (if we do), notions that remain gender based. According to the recently published *Janus Report on Sexual Behavior,* 87 percent of eighteen-to-twenty-six-year-olds surveyed believe that a double standard still exists. Virginity is still something that girls are supposed to cherish and save while red-blooded American boys should try desperately to lose. Many men still have some vague belief that they want to marry a virgin—someone who doesn't challenge their sense of adequacy, as one thirty-four-year-old man said to me, or someone, as Sigmund Freud speculated, over whom they can feel a sense of sole ownership. And many of the young women who answered are still very uneasy about coming to terms with their budding sexuality, allowing themselves to be talked into sex in order to be loved, feeling afterward that they've been degraded by or confused about the experience.

This fourteen-year-old junior high school student offers a typical reaction of younger women: "I didn't really think sex was a big deal, but it is. Maybe because my step-mom slept around a lot and cheated on my dad. She treated sex as nothing and was very promiscuous. So last year, when I was thirteen, I lost my virginity to a sixteen-year-old I had been friends with for three years. He was pretty drunk, and I had just broken up with my boyfriend of two years and was pretty upset. We went on a walk in the woods and lay down on his sweater. It hurt, and I bled a lot. I regretted it later and wished it had been with someone whom I was really in love with.

"I felt sad because losing my virginity should have been a wonderful experience, but instead it was meaningless. I let him inside of me, we were sharing something totally sacred, and it was treated as nothing. I felt like a slut, real dirty. I've had other sexual encounters since then. I feel that because my first time wasn't special, none of the other men I'm with will love me, and they'll think I'm dirty."

This conflict—is it acceptable for young women to have sex—finds its echo (and perhaps origins) in ideas we are exposed to in literature, movies, and television ads, through religion, and by parents and friends. We are given images of doe-like, innocent virgins, but when we turn the page or switch the channel we see a voluptuous, sensual, experienced women as the icon of female sex. Thus to be a virgin is both desirable and undesirable: You are fresh and marriageable; you are inexperienced and unappealing. To be sexually active is both desirable and undesirable: You are attractive, seductive, and comfortable with your sexuality; you've been around the block a few too many times. Within this maelstrom, each woman must find her place—and we do.

As one person said, "Sexuality is never far off from where I am spiritually," and this seemed to be true for many of us. No matter what their initial experience, as women learned to accept and value themselves as powerful and singular individuals, their sexuality blossomed. And in many cases, as they began to confront their sexual history, their very lives were transformed.

Ultimately, after reading all the questionnaires, what came across most strongly for me was the possibility of learning from each story. Although each response was unique and particular, each woman emerging as an individual, taken together they had a peculiar effect— no matter what the experience, there was something to discover, a shard of light that illuminated some aspect of

---

"Women in country music are either saints or sluts. She's either a 'good-hearted woman' or a 'honky-tonk angel.'"
                                                          —Molly Ivins

women's relationship to sexuality.

The questionnaire, serving as a platform, brought together all of the pain and joy and growth that we have shared in the act of speaking of our experience to form one strong, diverse voice—the voice of woman, coming to terms with her body and soul in all its complexity. Ideally we can use this awareness to be more sexually informed, to support our friends and sisters, to teach our daughters and sons. With understanding, education, and communication, we can create a context in which young women—and indeed all of us—can become empowered to make appropriate choices about their own sexuality.

The First Time is a result of many women sharing their most intimate stories. They have exposed a piece of themselves for others to see and in so doing, I believe, have done a service for us all.

Wedding Nights— or Almost

"A poignant piece of medical history, the 'lovers' knot,' illustrates the extreme measures taken by some women who are now in the grandmother age groups, in order to be virgins when they married. A 'lovers' knot' was a minor surgical procedure performed by some gynecologists between about 1920 and 1950. They would place several stitches in the labia of young women who were engaged and about to marry, and were not virgins. On their wedding night, when consummating their marriages, these women would feel pain, and bleed, convincing their new husbands that they were pure and virginal. Times change; to most Americans today, this procedure seems nothing short of barbaric. However, women endured it to satisfy the intense pressure placed on them to conform to the protocols of that time period."

–Samuel S. Janus, Ph.D., and
Cynthia L. Janus, M.D.,
The Janus Report on Sexual Behavior

Historically, women in this society were supposed to be virgins upon marriage. Virginity was considered a gift that a respectable woman offered her (usually sexually experienced) husband on their wedding night. Indeed women raised in the thirties and forties often equated virginity with their own worthiness to be a "good" wife, which was how women measured their value, in relation to a man. Frequently, this belief came from their father's opinions; as one woman stated, "My father told me that girls, `tramps,' who had sex, would never be wanted for wives by decent men."

"The act of defloration has been of greater psychological importance to men than it has ever been to women," claims Susan Brownmiller in *Against Our Will*. "When a husband 'deflowered' his wife on their wedding night, in terms of his pragmatic ideology he was breaking open a pristine package that now belonged to him—private property—and he wanted tangible proof of the mint condition of his acquisition."

Despite the fact that many of the influences dictating

women's proper sexual etiquette were male, the monitoring of behavior was often carried out by females. As Lillian Rubin in *Erotic Wars* explains, "Acceptance by other girls, an acceptance whose importance at this age transcended any concern about relationships with boys, required adherence to the sexual rules of the day. For although the rules may have been made by someone else, they were internalized by the girls who assumed responsibility for policing them."

That these attitudes and social rules have changed can be seen in how very few women responding to the questionnaire were virgins on their wedding night— three to be exact, all over the age of fifty. Even taking into account that those who would be more likely to hold to the standard would be less likely to respond to such a question, that's a very small percentage. It seems that wedding night virgins are a thing of the past.

The other women included here also first had sex with their husbands, but they didn't wait until their

---

"The high value which her suitor places on a woman's virginity seems to us so firmly rooted, so much a matter of course, that we find ourselves almost at a loss if we have to give reasons for this opinion. The demand that a girl shall not bring to her marriage with a particular man any memory of sexual relationship with another is, indeed, nothing other than a logical continuation of the right to exclusive possession of a woman, which forms the essence of monogamy, the extension of this monopoly to cover the past."
—*Sigmund Freud, "The Taboo of Virginity"*

wedding night; an engagement ring on their finger or promise of marriage was enough to permit themselves to have sex. Here, too, the youngest respondent was forty-eight, the rest in their fifties and sixties.

This fifty-two-year old white writer raised in Georgia tells a story that represents the ideal of the '50s (complete with an earlier molestation that she repressed for years): "I'm from a bygone era. I lost my virginity to my husband on my wedding night. I do not relate my experience with pride or with judgment about when the 'best' time and circumstances are. It's just that I was a southern girl from Atlanta, who grew up hearing sermons and Sunday school lessons about 'saving yourself' for your husband and not being 'damaged goods.' Back in the late 1950s, women were apparently comparable to merchandise. If even one man 'used' us, had sex with us, we were soiled, or seconds at best. (What about the men, I've often wondered, were they also used?)

"I was a compliant, nice girl, so I swallowed all this stuff whole. I felt passionately toward many of the young men I dated though I didn't have intercourse with any of them. We all did, however, get a lot of sexual mileage out of French kisses and slow dancing. Since many of us drew the line here, these pleasures were exquisite. I also liked to watch what we then viewed as sexy movies—James Dean in *Rebel Without a Cause* and Tab Hunter in *Battle Cry*. (I should point out that the pill was not widely used in 1958-59, and so part of my

waiting was also fear of pregnancy.) Though my husband-to-be and I had long, red-hot petting sessions that
came as close to intercourse as possible without actual
penetration, I was still technically a virgin in 1959 when
I walked down the aisle in a long white taffeta gown.

"I know my era was repressed yet I believe that now,
by seeing so much explicit sex in movies, and TV talk
shows geared to every sexual subject imaginable, we've
taken some of the wonderful mystery away. However,
even as I write this, I want to make it clear that I don't
think ignorance is bliss. I believe sexual ignorance is as
dangerous as sexual exploitation.

"Beginning with my husband's first tender kiss on
our second date, I knew he knew how to pleasure a
woman. I was right—our wedding night was great! No
doubt our lust was intensified by having waited so
long—we'd dated a year and a half. We used twelve
condoms that night, and the rest of the honeymoon was
almost as intense. Now, after thirty-two years together,
our chemistry, our attraction to each other, remains
strong.

"I did have one devastating 'sexual' experience just
before my marriage. My family doctor, a trusted family
friend and elder in our Presbyterian church, gave me a
'premarital exam' without a nurse present. (What for?
To see if all my parts worked?!) During the exam, he
pulled out a vibrator (I'd never seen one), told me he
needed to see if my responses were 'normal,' and then
proceeded to stimulate my clitoris with the vibrator,

bending over me, breathing heavily. I'll never forget his small brown eyes and neatly trimmed mustache. Looking back I see him as the embodiment of evil.

"I repressed this memory for a long time. Now I feel little guilt and much anger. My family and my religion drilled me not to question authority. And so, robot-like, I performed my duty of having a climax right there on the examining table. The doctor is still alive and only recently quit practicing. I never confronted the perverted SOB, but over the years I've grown to trust myself, and any man who would attempt sexual abuse now would be sorry. I only wish I could put my life in reverse long enough to deliver a karate kick in the balls that doctor would never forget."

A sixty-year-old housing counselor from New York also exemplifies her generation's ideals. "In the forties, when I came of age, petting, necking in the living room

---

"Virginity came in with a vengeance as every budding patriarch suddenly realized his divine right to a vacuum-sealed, factory-fresh vagina with built in hymenal gift-wrapping and purity guarantee . . . The highest value shifted from adult womanhood and pride of fecundity to maiden ignorance. Now the child bride, the unspoiled female, not-yet-woman, became the finest type; and a small film of atavistic membrane, the hymen, casually deposited by evolution in the recess of every woman's body, was discovered to be her prize possession."
—Rosalind Miles, *"The Women's History of the World"*

or in a car, was as far as we'd go. Yes, we had nymphos in the neighborhood, but they were not part of the 'preferred crowd.' A girl who slept around was a 'tramp.' We all knew who they were and usually felt sorry for them, not envious. Reputation, fear of being called 'loose,' keeping the boyfriend eager to see you again, betraying your parents' trust—all these were factors in one's sexual behavior.

"We knew about birth control, and condoms were commonly used, so fear of pregnancy was not the issue. By far, reputation and saving one's virginity for a special person whom we'd want to marry was of greatest importance. Virginity was the gift a girl presented to her husband to deflower.

"I started dating early, at age fourteen. By sixteen I had a very serious boyfriend whom I almost married. Sex without intercourse was always fun—to see how far we could go without 'doing it.' We came close many times but pulled away at the last moment. My boyfriends were all affectionate and sexy. I would date only guys I found physically attractive, smart, generous, and interesting. If someone disappointed me in any of the above, I didn't see him again. Of course, I was young, shapely, beautiful, and smart enough to know that if I chose the right mate, I had a chance of ensuring a good life (our mothers taught us this!).

"Virginity is a gift that you can give to your husband."
—*Catholic priest on the television show,*
Beverly Hills 90210

"As it happens, my husband—my deflowerer—didn't sexually satisfy me initially. He was young and inexperienced. We sought the help of a family doctor, who was very instructive and understanding and suggested ways I would find more exciting. He was a dear man who understood a woman's needs.

"Forty-one years later, sex remains an important component of our marriage. We are separated frequently and celebrate our reunions with loving times together. We kiss frequently during the day—more so than my children and their mates do!

"Growing up, I fell in love with most of the men I dated. Had it been the nineties, I would have been in bed with many guys at one time or another. I am still attracted to a lot of men of varying ages. But the thought of ever engaging in an extramarital affair has always been abhorrent to me—it is a betrayal of trust in my view. In the words of my great-grandmother (who recently passed away at ninety-two) upon learning that her granddaughter had lived with her boyfriend before marriage, 'If I had lived with your grandfather for two weeks before we took our vows, you can be certain I never would have married him!' In truth, hers was a rocky, mismatched marriage that probably shouldn't have happened. But folks were tough in those days, and relished the good times and repressed the bad times. I do believe past generations have been more unselfish and giving."

As these stories attest, women in their fifties and sixties have lived through, and had to contend with, tremendous social changes. A sixty-six-year-old white housewife details this struggle: "It was such a different time when I grew up! There were no talk-show hosts casually discussing infidelity, bizarre sex practices, or homosexual relationships—it just wasn't done. Sometimes, I think that the silence was better: that such things should be personal, intimate, and a person's own business. After all, what is more private than our sexuality? But I know that realistically, in these changing times, it is probably best that people air their dirty laundry so that things can progress. By things, I mean the elimination of men's violence towards women. Although I grew up sheltered, I am by no means completely ignorant. I know that women are raped all of the time. I also have some female friends who have begun to deal with childhood molestation. Before, perhaps, I would have never believed that these things happened, but because of my personal friends revealing their childhood (and adult) traumas, I know that something needs to change.

"I was fortunate enough to lose my virginity in a traditional, old-fashioned way—to my husband! We were so in love (he passed away recently), and the consummation of our marriage was a priceless moment that will always be imprinted as one of my fondest memories of him. Although our first time was not really physically satisfying, the gentleness, concern, and sensitivity was a wonderful display of all of the qualities I loved most about him. Never did his caring and concern for me diminish in forty-two years of marriage."

This fifty-one-year-old white woman from Louisiana didn't quite wait until the wedding night: "I had my first sexual intercourse with my fiance on New Year's Eve after attending a party and returning to a friend's apartment. My friend was out of town and the apartment was vacant, so it was quite easy. I was worried about getting pregnant because several of my friends had 'had' to get married and two risked illegal abortions.

"We had come very close several times prior to that night, but I resisted until I was sure we would be married. I was certainly ready for the experience, and it was extremely important to me that only the man who married me would deflower me. Six months later we broke up, and I was sure that everyone knew I was not a virgin anymore and therefore not a worthy woman.

"I told my new boyfriend I wasn't a virgin and I expected him to drop me since I was used merchandise. But he didn't, fortunately. Ironically, before a sexual encounter could occur with my new boyfriend, my former fiance and I reconciled and were married two months later.

The National Center for Health statistics for 1988 reports that approximately seventy percent of married American women have had premarital intercourse, and that by age twenty-five, ninety-five percent of American females have had sex.

"Having been a teenager in the 1950s, I had very limited sexual experience, mainly because I wore padded bras! I was extremely self-conscious about my small breasts. No amount of caressing, fondling, or kissing them contributed to sexual arousal until the birth of my daughter. I breast-fed her for about six months, and this seemed to have been the catalyst for removing my perceived stigma of small breasts. Also, birth-control pills weren't available, so of course I was terrified of getting pregnant and being shamed."

Some women of this generation took the opportunity offered by the changing times to redefine themselves. A therapist from Colorado in her early fifties demonstrates the low self-esteem often experienced by sexually inexperienced women, who blame themselves for their sexual shortcomings. "My first sexual experiences were with my husband—and they were not satisfying at all. I later discovered that he was not really attracted to me sexually. Therefore, I came to view myself as almost asexual and not at all appealing. It really never occurred to me that it might be something lacking in my husband or his basic attitude toward me—I just felt I must be doing something wrong.

"After my inevitable divorce, I was lucky enough to have a boyfriend whom I called my own personal Masters & Johnson team and whom my friends more rudely referred to as, 'The mad fucker of San Jose.' He had no sexual hang-ups, was an adroit and inventive lover, and believed I was a cute and desirable sex kitten. He introduced me to spontaneity and play in sex and was very instrumental in my becoming accepting and appreciative of my body, sensuality, and sexuality. This was my true introduction to sex."

Other women took sex as a matter of course, an inevitability that went hand-in-hand with long-term relationships and marriage. "I was twenty-six, a public school teacher and active member of a Methodist church," writes a forty-eight-year-old Texan. "I had male and female friends. I had my own apartment, but I worked and lived close to my parents, who were very important to me.

"I met Bobby through another teacher, who had him help us chaperon some school activities. We began to date and it was clear that sex was a large part of his life. I believe he was surprised to find a twenty-six-year-old virgin. When I saw that intercourse with him was inevitable, I went to my doctor and started birth control pills. I told the doctor that we were planning marriage, which at the time we were not.

"Bobby moved into my apartment. I don't recall our first intercourse encounter specifically but simply remember an ongoing sexual relationship. There was some physical pain the first few times, but it was not totally unpleasant. The mental and emotional turmoil of trying to keep my parents and the principal at my school from learning of our cohabitation was of much greater concern.

"We have now been married twenty-six years. We still have differences on sexual matters. He enjoys oral sex, but I do not. He would describe me as inhibited. Personally, I just do not see sex as a major component in my life except in my efforts to please my husband. He is a sexual expert, so I have orgasms regularly; these are wonderful.

"From viewing television talk shows and watching recent news, I'm beginning to feel that I'm of the minority who doesn't consider sex a central component of my life. It is a feel-good experience, but it is not the deciding factor in how I live and how happy I feel."

As these stories demonstrate, times have definitely changed. Just thirty years ago, the fear of becoming pregnant, being shunned, and never finding a man "who will take you," or being branded a fallen woman were real fears. But "then came the sixties and the sexual revolution. The restraints against sexual intercourse for unmarried women gave way as the Pill finally freed them from the fear of unwanted pregnancy. Seduction became abbreviated and compressed, oftentimes bypassed altogether, as women, reveling in their newfound liberation, sought the sexual freedom that had for so long been 'for men only'," as Lillian Rubin details.

Now young women have a different set of conflicts: on the one side, pressure from parents and, often, their church to abstain, and on the other, pressure from male partners to have sex compounded with peer pressure not to be stigmatized a virgin.

Pressure from All Directions

"Nevertheless, the way a young woman experiences her emerging adolescent sexuality depends very much on cultural standards and expectations. In the not-too-distant past, girls were taught to control themselves and not let the boys go too far. With the sexual revolution, some young girls are having sex much earlier, but most are still expected to exercise more self-control than boys in their sexual behavior."

—*Karen Johnson, M.D.*, Trusting Ourselves:
The Complete Guide to Emotional
Well-Being for Women

Pressure to have sex comes in many forms, some obvious and direct, others more subtle but no less effective. Traditionally, the pressure has come from the individual male—as Karen Johnson notes in the preceding quote, it was the boy's job to persuade and the girl's responsibility to resist. This timeless theme was evident in a great many of the stories. One young girl said specifically, "You want your boyfriend to continue liking you and you're afraid of the consequences of saying no." Some women seemed not to realize that they even had a choice: if their boyfriend wanted sex, that was that.

In many of these pressure situations, sex becomes a bargaining chip, a commodity to be given or withheld, which some girls see as a source of power that can have great allure to young women who perceive themselves as predominately powerless. A white salesperson from California claims she felt no pressure, but believes she lost her power when she lost her hymen. "When I was twenty, after going with my high school boyfriend for more than three years, I made the decision to finally say yes. I was very much in love with him and extremely comfortable and knew I had been driving him crazy after all that time of waiting. Although I never felt pressured, I felt a tinge of guilt because I couldn't explain why I didn't want to have sex with him. I think one of my fears for so long was that I would feel badly if we broke up. My virginity was one thing I would have even if we broke up. I didn't want to feel used up. After having sex for the first time, in his fraternity house, I did feel like I lost some power. Up until then it was the only thing I had of my own that I hadn't shared with him—that I could withhold."

Unlike previous generations, who hid their sexual activity for fear of being labeled "loose," a large number of these young women describe peer pressure to have sex: all of their friends were doing it, they didn't want to be left out. And although no one specifically referred to it, there is also *social* pressure to have sex—from advertising, television, and other media that present sexual activity in a glamorous light, a way to grow up, move away from childhood toward the attractions of adulthood.

In retrospect, the women in this chapter tended to feel emotionally uncomfortable about their first time, that perhaps they had done something wrong or had truly lost something of value. They struggle with the

---

"Virginity can be lost even by a thought."

—St. Jerome

fear of feeling taken advantage of and the notion of being used up. They seem particularly caught in the conflict between the old standard of virginity as a precious commodity and its antithesis—"everyone is doing it and so should you." Their ambivalence is neatly summed up by the following five stories.

"In a basement bedroom my boyfriend of three months and I, only fourteen, did it," remembers a twenty-four-year-old white salesperson from Kansas. "I was definitely nervous and unsure; he was ready and sure. I think he had to convince me somewhat, and once it happened it was fairly quick and painless. I felt kind of amazed afterward, but happy because it made him happy.

"Personally, I was a little let down by the whole sex experience. I didn't know my own body well and still don't. The experience lacked a turning-point quality. I still have never had an orgasm, and it never bothered me until now. I am engaged, and it has become somewhat of an issue with my fiance, who wants to know what he can do to please me. Since I am really not sure, we both become disappointed. Maybe my first experience set a precedent of sex with boyfriends—just being content that they're happy, but feeling indifferent and/or confused about my own physical satisfaction."

"I was sixteen, pressured by my boyfriend, but definitely curious about sex," writes a twenty-one-year-old black student from Kansas. "The entire episode seems a big blur, except that afterward I cried because it felt like someone had ripped out the inside of my vagina; I was swollen and sore and couldn't believe it was worth it. It was confusing to me that the purpose of sex was to feel great, because it was painful and seemed like a selfish, one-sided experience. Obviously, I wasn't ready physically or emotionally. The next day, on the telephone to my best friend, I announced that I hated sex and didn't want to do it anymore. I still feel the same way, although I keep having sex with my boyfriend."

"My boyfriend of nine months, who was also a virgin, told me one day when I was sixteen that he was ready for sex," recounts this nineteen-year-old student from North Carolina. "I told him I wasn't ready, and he was very understanding and said he could wait as long as I wanted. But he continued to bring up the subject and constantly asked me if I was ready yet! I cared about him very much but was scared of the words *fuck* and *sexual intercourse*. My body wasn't familiar to me, and sexually I felt unawakened.

"One night, when his parents were gone, I let him know that I thought I was ready; I guess all of his convincing paid off for him. We used a condom. It was awkward, and I was scared and didn't really enjoy it. I also didn't like the idea that it was so planned—no passionate spontaneity. My partner definitely enjoyed it, and our relationship took a big leap after intercourse;

we became a lot closer. It led me to feeling more confident about my body. My view of sex also changed; I thought people made a big deal about losing your virginity when in fact it didn't make you become a different person."

"I was in high school," recalls another college student from South Dakota. "I had been drinking, my inhibitions were down, just enough to help me relax, and the guy I had been dating for about three months began to pressure me. I guess I was talked into it. I wanted somebody to care for me and remember thinking that if I had sex with this guy, it would automatically mean something special. He used a condom, but I didn't even think about disease like everyone does now. Later I realized that just because you participated in a sexual act with someone, it didn't necessarily mean anything, unless emotions and communication are a part of it. For me and this guy, nothing monumental changed—it didn't make our relationship any stronger or deeper, only more awkward. I felt confused and later extremely hurt when I found out what a creep he was. I also felt very guilty; I knew I could not tell my mother because she would be upset and disappointed. I wished I could take back the experience.

"In college, I went out with a senior who wanted to sleep with me, but I wouldn't. He would stimulate me with his finger, and I knew so little about sex that I was confused as to why he did this. Now I know more about my body, but I still have never had an orgasm that I know of. I think that because my first sexual experience wasn't associated with love or intimacy, I disassociated the act from any feelings. Most of my sexual experiences have only been for pleasure not love."

This twenty-four-year-old white bookkeeper from Connecticut tells quite explicitly her reasons for succumbing to pressure: "I wasn't ready to have sex when I did, but I was afraid to tell my partner for fear of rejection and lack of acceptance. I knew he would be safe and delicate, but neither my body nor my heart was in it. I didn't know what to expect, I wasn't sexually educated. I was scared and felt nervous—very typical, I guess. When I got home, I cried and felt dirty, because I knew it was something my parents would be disgraced by—or so I thought at the time.

"The experience did inhibit future relations, because I didn't want to feel insecure and uncomfortable again, until I fell in love with someone for the first time. With him, it truly felt like making love; I enjoyed it for the first time and felt my sexuality slowly and tentatively awakening. My body seemed attractive to him, thus I felt attractive—and like a woman for the first time.

"Another interesting sexual revelation came when I went away to college. My roommate was a very butch type—not someone whom I was sexually attracted to (not to mention that she was a woman!) at first. But after continuous advances, I began to feel something toward her that changed my perception of sexuality. I realized I had been awakened to a new frontier, which I haven't explored since then, but am glad to have been introduced to."

Some women reported being maneuvered into bed through words. Because they desperately wanted emotional connection, they were often ready to believe what a man said, even if he were a stranger, as this thirty-three-year-old Hispanic writer acknowledges: "My first experience was humiliating. I was nineteen years old and from a small town in New Jersey. I went away from home for the first time, to a big city for a school convention. I was staying at a fancy hotel with my cousin. It was only a month after I graduated from high school. Back home, I had a steady boyfriend, but I must have been looking for something more exciting.

"One of the nights on the trip, I met a stranger. He told me wonderful things: how beautiful I was, how sexy, how intelligent. We kept drinking wine and talking all through the night. He told me that if he were my lover, he'd treat me like a queen. I bought the whole thing.

"It wasn't love we made. It was so much more violent. I was a virgin and he tore me to bits. Blood all over the sheets; sores on my neck. I felt really cheap. I saw him much later at a party, and he didn't even acknowledge me. Two months later, I found out I was pregnant from him. I never made love to my boyfriend back home; I never even saw him again. I worked as a camp counselor during the summer to pay for the abortion. My father thought I was nothing but a cheap, dirty whore and told me men only married virgins.

"After that experience, I met a boyfriend in college, whom I think I loved. He was smart and funny. We had total sex: the more we had the better. Wow! The pity was that I never let him close to me emotionally. I was like a solid, brick wall—a fortress protecting my heart. This hurt him. I always put up barriers when we really started to talk and feel close—when I felt he was starting to probe into my soul—then I would back way off. I thought if I let him in, he'd crush me completely. I have never been truly open or free with men."

Several women report being pressured by much older men; this thirty-year-old white receptionist was only fourteen: "In my freshman year of high school, a friend's brother started taking an interest in me. He was twenty-one, had been a medic in Vietnam, and drove a Triumph Spitfire. Needless to say, I was thoroughly impressed that he liked me.

"We dated three months before I lost my virginity. My mom had to go to an AA meeting about sixty miles away, and my brother and I were left alone for the weekend. The first night we attempted to have sex, it was a failure; he couldn't get a hard-on—he was probably stoned on pot. I took it very personally, but the next night we tried again and succeeded. Afterward, I felt basically nothing—it was certainly not wonderful or earth-shattering. He was just interested in popping my cherry, and we quit seeing each other immediately after that. Because he was older, and I thought he expected it, I had definitely felt pressured to have sex with him and feel that he took advantage of my naivete.

I also think I had a skewed image of what it meant to be intimate with someone because I had been molested at age five by an older brother. I don't remember exactly what happened, only that it did. I do remember that I was paralyzed with fear and that his wife was passed out in their bed. I finally got out a yelp, and he left me alone. It's no wonder that, until last year, I tended to use sex as a weapon, and not view it as a mutual experience. My first encounter only reaffirmed that unless a man wanted me sexually, I was basically worthless. It's very sad to me that I spent so much time and energy try to make men want me."

A black social worker, thirty-one, felt coerced by an older man, an authority figure, but her experience was more physically positive. "Looking back on my first time, I feel a combination of being taking advantage of and desperately needing to feel loved. I grew up in a rough neighborhood and lived with my single mother who worked incredibly hard to raise me properly and keep me off the streets. But because she worked so hard, she had little energy left to spend lots of time with me. As an only child, with no grandparents or father, it seemed like I was just a small, insignificant speck on the planet—very alone. So when a teacher at school began to flirt with me—a young, attractive man whom all of the girls had a crush on—I was flattered, felt chosen, and was thirsty for the attention. A sixteen-year-old shouldn't be deflowered by her teacher though; I was just a baby. But it takes two to tango, and I was more than willing.

"As far as first times go, it was probably better than most. He was twenty-seven and experienced, and knew how to be gentle and tender. My friends sometimes shared horrifying stories of seventeen-year-old male egos, trying to pretend they were experienced, and not ever wanting to please or talk to the woman about her satisfaction. At least this teacher cared about me and wasn't rough."

This white teacher in her thirties from Oregon was persuaded by the logic of inevitability to have her first time with an older man: "One day when I was seventeen, an older male friend said to me, 'You know, you're going to have to lose your virginity sooner or later. And I care for you, so why not me?' Believe it or not, I bought it. He put it so logically.

"A few days later, he invited me to dinner. We spent the evening talking, about ourselves, our lives, and the entire time I kept getting more and more distant—further out of my body. Because I knew intercourse with him was inevitable, I was preparing myself mentally by disassociating my heart and body. I knew I wasn't in love with this person. It felt like I was complying, and I'm not sure why I did.

"It wasn't until I met a woman several years later that I came back into my body and bells went off. But I consider myself bisexual, not a lesbian."

Here a forty-seven-year-old businesswoman from Oklahoma recalls her seduction by an older male and the later blossoming of her sexuality: "I was only thirteen, had just started dating, and had no idea how to flirt. Petting and kissing didn't turn me on; in fact, I simply put up with it. But he was turned on, this guy I was dating. He must have been eighteen or nineteen, much older than me. He worked as a sacker in the grocery store; I worked as a food demonstrator. We went to a drive-in movie, then to park at an isolated spot in the boonies. When he was hard, he put my hand on his penis, through his jeans, and told me how much he needed me. He was breathing heavy and feeling me all over, started fumbling with my clothes, and I just let it progress to the end. I remember bleeding, but there was no pain, except for the pain of intercourse without lubrication from arousal, which actually is pretty uncomfortable.

"You budding virgin, fair and fresh and sweet, whither away, or where is thy abode? Happy the parents of so fair a child; Happier the man, whom favourable stars allot thee for his lovely bed fellow."
        —William Shakespeare, *"The Taming of the Shrew"*

"Later, I felt let down and sorry that I had had sex, because I didn't want to be talked about and snickered over. I knew I'd lost a potentially meaningful experience, a time I'd never get back.

"I continued to be sexually active until I became pregnant at fifteen; my folks got an abortion for me. I married at seventeen, and the sex was just something I let happen to me. But at twenty-two, I met a man who absolutely turned me on, and we had an affair, for about a year. I continued to stay married to my husband, however, and after the affair was monogamous until I was twenty-eight. When I met a forty-one-year-old man who spoke to my heart, I realized how superficial our marriage had always been. I truly fell in love, had a wonderful affair of the heart, soul, and body, and divorced my husband and married my true love. For eighteen years now, we've had the most wonderful love; he awakened me to how real love and sex worked."

Many women felt that once they had been pressured into something they hadn't consciously chosen, the right to make a decision seemed frivolous. They no longer felt that what they wanted mattered. Here's a white twenty-eight-year-old from Tennessee: "When I was in high school, I naively considered penetration to be the ultimate sexual experience. Not wanting to deny myself this pleasure, I masturbated with a water-filled bottle. It was lousy, ridiculous, and it hurt.

"When I entered college, I lived in a dormitory with

several other women who had sex whenever they chose to with no apparent thought of the consequences. Earlier, I had known women who had gotten pregnant, but all of my friends in high school were virgins and had no boyfriends. In college, I met up with a group of women who experimented with sex and marijuana. It was all very strange to me. At the time, although I thought it was wonderful that youth could take part in something that is—and shouldn't be—taboo, I was still suspicious about their motives. I thought that maybe they were faking their sophistication.

"That year, I tried everything they did, including sex. There were certainly plenty of interesting women around, but I thought that my chances of finding a lesbian were about zero. There were also a few interesting men, none of whom were interested in initiating me.

"In the beginning of the school year, I had briefly met a student from Nigeria. In the spring I ran into him, and he was surprised that I remembered his name. He walked me to my dorm, where he surprised me by pinching my breast. Nobody had ever touched me, even in a less intimidating fashion, so I was shocked. Some voice inside of me said, 'This is where it's going to take place.'

"At the time, I was flunking out and was extremely depressed. I believed that my only asset was my intelligence, and I had just gotten kicked out of honors' college. I had turned away from my classmates out of humiliation and was taking more drugs, which were expensive, and as a result I didn't have enough money for tuition. Needless to say, I was hitting rock bottom.

"On the bed in my dorm room, he began rubbing me. Later, we got up and went to his house. There was no foreplay and a lot of drool. It hurt; he did use a condom, however. His roommate came in and was surprised to see me, even though there was a note in the kitchen intended for his eyes only. It said: 'I brought a friend home. A few pushings, nothing serious (white).'

"The first night he penetrated four times. I hated it. I told him no after the first time, but it didn't seem to make much difference anymore. I figured that after this experience, I wouldn't have heterosexual sex anymore, but I did several times.

"I did have luck when I was twenty; I met somebody with whom I had a lot in common. He liked me and we got married. I really didn't want to—it's so corny. But I'd never had a good relationship with anybody my whole life. I thought I had friends, but I don't think they ever really cared about me. I think that most people do not like unattractive people because they make them feel inferior. But I know that this man cares about me. This man, who is heterosexual, wishes he were a lesbian. He is kind and ensures my orgasm. It doesn't hurt. It even feels good. I'm still not sure whether heterosexual sex can ever be pleasurable. I have someone who is passive, which is better than aggressive, but it is an odd bedroom life based on love and hugging and experimentation.

"I used to think I was bisexual, but now I think it's more complex than that. For one thing, I find I like more traditionally male stuff, such as science fiction, politics, and biology. Actually, I think I'm asexual, though I wouldn't mind having a relationship with a woman I could relate to."

As the preceding story illustrates, often there is only a fine line separating pressure and date rape. The following story, by a twenty-three-year-old Korean saleswoman from Illinois, embodies the ambiguities: manipulation, coercion, and non-consensuality are all factors. "My first full-blown sexual intercourse took place on a second date with a man nine years older than me. I was inebriated and knew we would fool around, but I had no plans on having intercourse with him.

"He undressed me and began undressing himself. I told him not to—I didn't want us both to be naked. He kept saying 'Relax . . . ' Creepy.

"He lived with his parents, and I was conscious of the fact that they were upstairs. I didn't want them to wake and find me there, and I also didn't want to have sex with him. I felt completely, utterly vulnerable. He used a condom, so I didn't fear pregnancy or disease, but I remember feeling nervous and, later, ashamed. I tried to fool myself into thinking I wanted it because it would make it easier on everyone if I did. But it didn't.

"Oddly enough, after this I overcame my hyperconsciousness of my body image. From fourteen to twenty-one, I was extremely image conscious. I was bulimic from fifteen to seventeen, and before losing my virginity, I was on a strict regime: 1,000 calories a day, running five to ten miles a day. I realized that I was dangerously close to becoming bulimic/anorexic again, and I decided to stop counting calories but continue the exercising. When I felt at peace with myself physically, my sexuality began to flourish and I fell in love.

"I consider myself to be a very sexually oriented person and find energy in sex appeal. When I eventually began a loving sexual relationship, it allowed me to express myself in powerful yet subtle ways. I also had my first orgasm with a partner. Up until then I thought I could only achieve orgasm through masturbation. I realized being more aggressive (in all realms, not just sex) made me feel much more attractive—and happy."

This white twenty-two-year-old student from Nebraska was scared into having sex with her boyfriend for fear of his violent reaction if she refused: "I remember distinctly that two weeks before my first sexual experience my mother gave me a talk about sex, because I had just turned sixteen. She told me how I needed to be careful because most guys just wanted sex. I had been seeing one of 'those' guys for three months. When we were alone, we would kiss and touch each other's

---

After two high school students in Milford, Utah compiled a roster of 160 classmates they believed to be virgins, teacher Cherry Florence read the list to her class.

genitals. He gradually worked up to asking me if we could have sex. I didn't want to so I told him no. The first couple of times I said no, he just sighed and acted a little upset, but then forgot it.

"After a while, when I refused, he would get really upset and make a scene: He would hit things and slam objects down on a dresser, and such. By this time I was scared of him. Finally, one day when we were alone in his room, he asked me again. Because I was scared of him and no one else was home, I just gave in. I didn't enjoy it at all. It hurt mostly, and I just lay there. I didn't feel much of anything after it was over except humiliation and shame, because I was brought up to believe that sex was for marriage. I continued to have sex with him for three to four months. I figured since I had already given in once, I couldn't say no again. When I look back on it, I hate myself for being so naive and I also hate him. I know I shouldn't blame myself because I was coerced and fearful.

"When I later encountered other sexual situations with other men, I always said no. Most of the guys took no for an answer, but there were a few, one or two, who were able to manipulate me into having sex. After these experiences, I felt ashamed and guilty again and told myself that I have to be in control and not let guys do that to me.

"Because of these experiences I had a negative view about sex so I turned away from it. It took a wonderful man to bring about a turning point in my sexuality. Now

I truly know what it means to be loved and how to love sexually. My partner takes care of my needs as well as his own. I have become orgasmic while having penile-vaginal intercourse for the first time. I don't think of sex as a duty, but as a way of expressing the way I feel about my partner. I don't feel guilty, ashamed, or dirty anymore. I am grateful to him for helping me experience real love."

Not surprisingly, many of these "pressured into it" stories come from women who reported childhood sexual abuse or early harassment. Perhaps because of their earlier experience, their notion of sexual free will is impaired, as this thirty-four-year-old white Protestant from Massachusetts implies:

"At age twelve I was obsessed with a boy at school who was really a 'bad boy.' He was into drugs, had a criminal record, was older than me (seventeen), and was hard-looking. I had almost no knowledge of or interest in sex. He eventually got the message that I 'liked' him from my friends and asked me to come over to his house; he lived in a housing project with his parents. In his room, with his parents' knowledge, we smoked an outrageous amount of pot, to the point that I was obliterated and only loosely in contact with myself. I remember three things: his body on top of me, a moment of pain, and wetness. I had no idea what we had done, or even what to call it!

"Before then, I never understood what it was all

about, even to the point of blocking out earlier 'sexual experiences.' I remember some inappropriate fondling by older men that simply seemed gross at the time, like eating cauliflower would have been, I guess, except that I was instructed not to mention those experiences, which made me feel like it was my fault and that I'd done something wrong. I vaguely remember something with police involvement, but I never understood what really happened.

"It wasn't until two years later that I began to become more enlightened about sex. Now I realize that all of my sexual activity was initiated (when I felt I was consenting) for the purpose of getting attention from men. I didn't feel interested in it until I reached my twenties, though I had been consistently sexually active since age fourteen. When I was nineteen, I had a sexual experience with someone who loved me—it was amazing; I cried the whole time. I did have an orgasm once when I was fourteen; not surprisingly, I didn't know what had happened, and it wasn't until I was thirty-three that I had an orgasm with a partner again."

Younger and younger women now feel the pressure to have sex, to be experienced and worldly. Despite safe-sex education, everyone from friends to television is saying: "Just do it." This twenty-one-year-old white student from Illinois explains:

"I was the last virgin in my close group of friends, and I admit that I did feel pressure from my peers. The first time was enjoyable, but awkward. I felt physically worn out but satisfied with what took place; I wouldn't change a thing. Overall, it did give me a sense of power. I tend to like being in control, and, during sex, I enjoy being in the power position, so to speak."

A black teacher's aide from Oklahoma details another situation where peer pressure and pressure to be "grown up" influenced her decisions. "Over the Thanksgiving holiday when I was seventeen, I went with a friend to my cousin's college. We knew there would be something going on because the athletes would be there for the weekend games. We were just hanging around in my cousin's dorm room when some basketball players came. After they left, my cousin asked me if I was interested in any of them. I said that one of the guys was all right; I guess she told him on the sly. In the meantime, we began to drink. Later, the guy, Roger, came back for me. He asked me if I was drunk, and I said I knew what I was doing. He did ask me if I had protection.

"It was the most fucked up night of my life. He did not even fully undress me, and never even kissed me. I don't know if the pain was more physical or emotional, but it hurt. After he finished, he got up and took a shower. When he came back, he saw that there was blood on the sheets, and he asked me why I didn't tell him I had my period. (It was blood from my hymen being broken!) I said, 'Why didn't you ask?' Then he asked me if I knew the way back to my cousin's dorm, and I left.

"After this experience, I didn't have sex for a year and a half. I hated it. I thought it was overrated. I had not experienced romance or a good kind of pain. I felt guilty and humiliated. I was ashamed that I let peer pressure make a decision for me that I wasn't ready for.

"I just recently had my first intimate love, where his feelings were the same as mine. I finally got romance and that good kind of pain. He cooked breakfast for me in the morning. I was made to feel wanted."

Here's a thirty-two-year-old white woman from Indiana, who tells her story as though her mother's counseling her against being sexually active actually pressured her into it: "I was smitten by a boy my brother brought home from his Catholic boarding school. Mark had wild, curly blond hair. He was a self-proclaimed authority on women's behavior and appearance; because he had two older sisters who shared their secrets with him. My older sister and I competed for his attention. While she could amuse him with her wit, I would try to attract him with my adolescent beauty; I was about fourteen. He visited frequently in the summers.

"One night we were all drinking wine out back by the pool. Somehow, we ended up in my bedroom on my bunk bed. As we were lying there, my head spinning from alcohol, my father walked in and caught us. Shortly thereafter, my mother came in to have a chat with me about pregnancy and not disappointing my father. This episode set the stage for the inevitable 'big night.'

"My brother decided that I could join him to visit Mark and his family, who lived in the Chicago suburbs. I was in awe of his older sisters; one wore incredibly high platform shoes. That night, my brother left Mark and me alone. I think I had drunk some wine. I remember that sex with him was passionless and insensitive. I remember feeling moisture in my vagina after he had entered me. I was touching the wetness and remarked, 'What is this?' He put me off and embarrassed me by saying, 'It's nothing. You'll laugh about it later.'

"I felt shameful about the whole incident. Afterward, I didn't feel the same about Mark, mostly disappointed. I guess I felt used by him and even my brother, who had knowingly set me up.

"Three months later, I was driven back to Chicago. This time, Mark and his wise sisters had set up what they called a 'menstrual suction' or something like that. It was reasoned to be not as bad as an abortion; it was supposedly a procedure that would simply start up your period again. I seriously don't know if I was pregnant or if I just went along with it out of fear. My father had always said that if any of us—there were four daughters—got pregnant, we were out the door.

"After losing my virginity, I didn't have any more sexual encounters until I met my high school sweetheart. At a time of insecurity and uncertainty, he was my Rock of Gibraltar. I don't think I ever had a true orgasm with him, though; I still felt mixed up when it came to physical intimacy. When I met my husband many years later, after numerous meaningless sexual relationships, I still felt as though I had to perform for him. Finally, though, we have reach an understanding in our lovemaking. If I am not satisfied, the whole experience is less for both of us. I am not only physically satisfied with my husband, but mentally and intellectually at peace. I feel the love and care with him that I lacked for so many years with so many men. I can verify the rumor that women get more sexual as they get older."

Many women who had a strict religious upbringing felt particularly torn about their sexual initiation. Jewish women were often expected to date only Jewish men; Southern Baptists were taught that sex was solely for marriage. In particular, Catholic women who filled out questionnaires often spoke of the conflicting pressure between Church teachings—and parental morals—and their own desires. Because they were taught that what they were doing was wrong (even though they did it regardless), the women respondents often became cut off from open communication with their parents and the Church, both of which they often wanted to remain close to.

This thirty-five-year-old white teacher raised in California explains the emotional turmoil she was put through when trying to simultaneously appease her mother, the Church, her curiosity, and her boyfriend.

"After eight months of discussions and excuses, I caved in to the pressure. As eighteen-year-old senior in high school, I think I was the last virgin left out in my large group of sexually active friends. A friend's mother, who communicated responsibly with her daughter about sex, helped me with birth control. Because of my Catholic upbringing and my mother's vehement crusade against abortion, I was terrified of getting pregnant, not to mention the Church teachings that birth control was wrong and that sex was strictly for procreation. How archaic and patriarchical! I hid my birth-control pills inside a Tylenol package, in a plastic make-up bag, under the sink, and behind the toilet paper in my own bathroom. I couldn't imagine what would happen if I got caught. I wished desperately, then and now, that I could have talked with my mother about it and not felt like I had to lie. (But in retrospect, and looking at my relationship with her now, I think that she doesn't really want to know the truth: She would rather hold on to fairy tales, like that my father hasn't been an alcoholic for the past twenty years and that my brother isn't a pathological liar and drug user.)

"The actual event was very anticlimactic; I basically just wanted to get it over with and find out what everybody thought was so great! Not surprisingly, my first partner was aggressive and unloving. He didn't try hard to satisfy me, probably due to his own lack of experience which led to insecurity. He was selfish, and I always felt like he was doing it for himself and didn't care about communicating with or satisfying me. My next partner, to whom I am now engaged, has shown me the true meaning of making love: communication, trust, tenderness, sharing, and passion. I feel tremendously lucky to have found him.

"I'm still one of the many trying to come to terms with sex and the Church. And my mother."

A Catholic bank teller in her twenties tells of how her life was affected by the guilt she felt. "To be totally honest, I remember very little. I know he never ejaculated, but I was still stunned. He just sort of left. I was embarrassed because I thought he was disappointed with me. This had a huge impact on my life. I was somewhat embarrassed about my body. I had never trusted anyone enough to become involved in a sexual relationship. I believed that sex was something you shared only with someone you loved. Marriage was required, but unfortunately I settled for engagement instead. I felt somewhat guilty about the fact that I didn't wait, but now I enjoy sharing myself with my partner."

This twenty-six-year-old Catholic Hispanic felt guilt and blamed the pressure of love for "making" her do it: "It was great; I was in love. We were together for two

---

I will say it boldly, though God can do all things, He cannot raise a virgin up after she has fallen.

—St. Jerome, "De Virginitie"

years before we did it, and I felt a lot of Catholic guilt, but love made me do it. He was a quite older black man, and I barely spoke English at first; I had just come from Mexico and was twenty-three when we did it for the first time. He wanted to marry me—he was very old-fashioned and totally respected and loved me. Afterward, though, I always felt like I was going to be punished in some way."

Of course, you certainly don't have to be Catholic to feel guilty about sex, as this thirty-four-year-old Presbyterian minister points out: "My high school boyfriend and I had been sweethearts from the fifth grade on. When I was fifteen, we were in love and spontaneously one day, after having lusty fooling-around sessions for years, we had sex. Afterward, guilt overwhelmed me, and I unfairly blamed him. In fact, I kissed another boy right in front of him eight hours later, because I wanted to hurt him. I did, and he spent the night crying in the woods! I was physically ready, because I had started my period when I was nine, but emotionally not mature enough. I felt dirty because I had been taught that nice girls don't have sex. Because of my guilt about sex, my body wasn't awakened until college. Then my attitude about sex went from feeling guilty about it to enjoying it and manipulating men with it."

Like the preceding woman, this forty-eight-year-old psychologist from Colorado felt pressured to have sex, then quickly learned that it was a way to gain power over men: "Coming from a very religious and sexually repressive family, I lacked any knowledge about sex, but I was tired of fighting the battle to remain a virgin and felt pressured by most of my high school boyfriends. So, when I was eighteen I made the decision to have sex. Of course, the major problem was that I knew absolutely nothing about it. I was in denial and didn't think pregnancy would happen to me and took no precautions. As a result, I got pregnant, and my boyfriend of about a year and I got married. I felt shamed by my first sexual experience and did not enjoy it at all.

"Although my family never discussed sex, I was always curious and open about all feelings, including the sexual ones. The modus operandi of my dysfunctional family was: Don't talk, don't trust, don't feel. Therefore, my curiosities were explored on the sly. When I was discovered playing "I'll show you mine if you'll show me yours" when I was very young, I was severely punished. (The boy went unpunished.) I learned that sex could feel good by having my dog lick my clitoris. But I was about thirty-four before I ever achieved an orgasm while having intercourse. I always thought that something was wrong with me because I could only have an orgasm by manipulation.

"But the discovery of sex gave me a sense of magical power over men. My family promoted, to some degree, the belief that men were the dominant sex and somehow superior. Sex seemed to be a method to gain the upper hand occasionally. Unfortunately, I began to view it as a tool, not as a process to be enjoyed, and didn't begin to explore my true sexuality until I got divorced and joined a women's support group. The safety of this environment lead me to discover the depths of my womanhood."

Manipulating men through sex was a theme of several women in this chapter. One woman in her thirties wrote, "I have spent my whole life using sex as a powerful tool to control the men in my life. It took me a long time to realize that I was playing the same game that men do (loving and leaving), instead of being involved in a mutually satisfying relationship where nobody has the upper hand." Because these women felt pressured to have sex, they then perceived sex as an exploitation and proceeded to turn the tables against men, the very people who had pressured them in the first place, using them as they felt they had been used.

Women who did not feel pressured had a wholly other view of sex. For them, it was an experience to partake in freely, and virginity was something to be given freely.

A Conscious
Choice

"Sexual activities for the female before marriage were proscribed in ancient codes primarily because they threatened the male's property rights in the female whom he was taking as a wife. The demand that the female be virgin at the time of her marriage was comparable to the demand that cattle or other goods that he bought should be perfect, according to the standards of the culture in which he lived."

—*Alfred Kinsey, et al,*
Sexual Behavior in the Human Female

We've come a long way since the days when women were considered the property of men. Women are no longer required to come to the marital bed hymen intact and slowly Western culture has begun to shed other inequitable ideas of sexuality. Birth control, feminism, and the reevaluation of the sexual double standard have combined to offer women the option of choosing when and how and with whom to first have intercourse.

"We need only look at the difference in the sexual histories of the forty-year-olds and twenty-year-olds to see how deeply the transformation in sexual norms we have witnessed has been integrated into the culture, consolidated into sexual behavior and internalized by the majority of adults, as well as teenagers, in the country," wrote Lillian Rubin five years ago in *Erotic Wars*, her study of the effects of the sexual revolution on society.

Because of these changing mores, most of the respondents who planned their first time were younger. Growing up in a time when feminism was forcibly ushered into the mainstream, the women in these stories claim their right to be sexual beings. Unlike many of their peers in the previous chapter, they didn't need to be talked into sex by their partner; it was something they wanted. Nonetheless, these women often still feel conflicted about how they should be in relation to their sexuality. They are trying to sort out contradictory messages among media, parents, religion, and peers to decide what is right for them. One way to deal with the complexities of the experience is to focus on logistics.

Indeed, as the following stories show, many young women now plan, sometimes with painstaking detail, the first time with their boyfriends. They take birth-control pills a month before in anticipation of the event. They notice when parents will be gone and conspire with each other to plan romantic trysts—condoms included. Girls seem to be educated early on about birth control and sexually transmitted diseases; even if they're not careful, they're aware of the risk.

What is particularly interesting about these planned events is that so many of the women who report this experience complain about the quality of the sex itself, as if planning to have sex and knowing how to have good sex are the same thing. These stories, more than most others, often mention the physical pain of first intercourse. A twenty-one-year-old student from Kansas offers a typical tale.

"Since I was raised as a Catholic, and Catholics believe that it is a sin to have sex before marriage, that had a great influence on my experience. When I was sixteen, I got curious—all of my friends were talking about sex—and decided I wanted to try it. A guy I had known for about four years, my best friend's brother, was the one I decided on. I was physically attracted to him and felt fairly safe. We got semi-drunk. I remember that it was very painful. I was so nervous. I felt uncomfortable, that I was doing something wrong.

"Afterward I felt weird around him, like it shouldn't have happened. I didn't enjoy it because of the pain, and the disappointment of wanting it to be so special and it turning out disastrously. It also seemed like my body wasn't even involved—I was numb to the whole experience. I wondered if something was wrong with me because my friends didn't talk about sex in this way. I'm still waiting to feel comfortable with sex and feel so nervous that it always turns out horribly. I think I just feel too much pressure to have the perfect experience."

"It was completely, entirely planned," says another twenty-one-year-old from Illinois. "I had arranged to be

---

A European marriage custom of the fourteenth century required the newlywed couple to be escorted to the marital bed by family members and the priest, who offered a blessing prior to consummation of their union. The bloody bed sheet was displayed the morning after as proof of a successful sexual encounter and the wife's virginity.

on the pill and my boyfriend had been checked out for possible STDs from a prior experience. We planned it for Friday the thirteenth, which I thought would be humorous to remember. We had been sexually experimenting in other ways for a long time, so the buildup to the event that evening was great! However, the actual act really sucked. It hurt. I endured the pain only because I had the understanding that it would get better—it did about six times later. It was not what I had expected in terms of my emotional experience; I was disappointed because my partner fell asleep soon afterward without any discussion or cuddling. Otherwise, I didn't feel different or that I'd experienced a rite of passage.

"It's sort of the same feeling one gets on birthdays: you know you're a year older, but you don't feel it. Maybe I felt relieved to be a member of the 'nonvirgins' club; if the topic of sex came up, I could now have my own stories and not feel so naive. It took me a long time to get the guts to ask my partner for what I wanted, which in retrospect is rather upsetting that I didn't have the confidence to communicate my needs to my partner."

Often, women felt independent and powerful when planning their own experience, because they were making the decision to have sex, on their own, in a responsible way. "It was a big plan I'd had for a while," relates this twenty-four-year-old Californian. "My parents were leaving for the weekend, so I told my boyfriend and he decided he would spend the night. We were really excited and didn't tell anyone except my best friend, who was the decoy—she was supposedly spending the night with me. Actually, I only told her not to spend the night but didn't even tell her why! Therefore it seemed like a clandestine adventure, and I was responsible for making it happen.

"He brought several condoms. We felt both devious and mature at the same time. After fooling around for a while, he tried to enter me, but probably due to my nervous excitement and inexperience, I was not at all lubricated. Therefore, it hurt like HELL—I will never forget the pain. It seemed like we tried for hours, never quite succeeding, with me whining about the soreness. Finally we went to sleep. The next morning we were determined to make it happen, and although I was incredibly sore, he was able to go in all the way—I think. He was so happy when he was inside me, and I felt happy that it was so important to him.

"It felt like a bold, independent move on my part because I had decided on my own that it was the right time. Up until then, my life had been very prescribed by what was expected of me. I felt confident and happy about my decision but, unfortunately, it had an upsetting end result. About three months later, I thought I was pregnant and confided in my mother. Family crisis ensued, because she told my father. Rumors, bitterness, anger, and guilt followed, even after I learned that I wasn't pregnant. I didn't have sex again for four years. The feelings of responsibility, maturity, and happiness quickly faded and were difficult to recover."

Some women planned to have sex not necessarily because they physically desired to, but because they felt it was a form of rebellion, like this twenty-two-year-old Catholic waitress from Missouri: "My boyfriend of two years, my first love at age sixteen, had wanted to have sex for a long time, but I wasn't sure—I was really scared that it would hurt. The night we had sex for the first time, we had planned and discussed it beforehand. My parents were out of town, and we had sex in my own bed. It was very painful, and I did not have a good time at all—I bled the whole time and just wanted to get the painful part over with. He held me tightly afterward and made me feel very loved. Although my body felt uncomfortable and sore, I felt emotionally satisfied and closer to my partner than ever before; it was his first time also.

I felt it was more 'the thing to do' than a pleasurable, intimate experience. I never reached an orgasm with him; it seemed like the pleasure was all his. I did feel a sense of independence because I was doing something

---

"Are there still virgins? One is tempted to answer no. There are only girls who have not yet crossed the line, because they want to preserve their market value ... call them virgins if you wish, these travelers in transit."

—Francoise Giroux

that was highly regarded as wrong in my religion and my school, which was a private, Catholic girl's school."

In all of these stories, women were very aware of and educated about birth control. What they seemed to have not discussed or known about was how their own bodies would respond. They were largely unaware of their own capacity for physical pleasure, which is not surprising. As the Januses point out in *The Janus Report on Sexual Behavior*, "The open discussion and study of sexuality dates back only about a century, to the work of Sigmund Freud," and there is still much more acceptance of sexual experimentation—especially masturbation—for boys than for girls.

Women even learn more about male sexuality than their own, notes Karen Johnson in *Trusting Ourselves*. "Ironically, many women know more about male genital anatomy than they do about their own. A great deal of a woman's ability to enjoy her own sexuality depends on how she feels about her body and how much she knows about her sexual organs. Unfortunately, few women feel completely satisfied with the appearance of their bodies. This lack of self-acceptance certainly has negative effects on their sexual pleasure."

Here's a twenty-six-year-old writer from California who came to realize that the problem was not with her, but with a lack of proper sex education: "One day during my senior year in high school, my first boyfriend and I snuck off to his parent's cabin with the intent to be romantic. We became physical and I wanted to have sex, but my boyfriend was an incredibly responsible person and said no (this time). A few weeks later, in celebration of getting my braces off, we planned another encounter, very carefully, birth control included.

"We met at my parent's house and all I can remember is that it was incredibly painful and very bloody. Nobody told me it was going to hurt that bad. All I kept thinking was—just get it over with! Not a romantic thought. After losing my virginity, I thought that I was frigid for the next two years because I could never orgasm or really enjoy sex. Taking a human sexuality class really opened my eyes! I learned how to masturbate and discovered the pure joy of orgasm. My first orgasm wasn't with a guy, but with myself. I wasn't able to enjoy my body with someone else until I learned a little more about it myself. No longer is *frigid* part of my vocabulary, only mis-education."

This twenty-one-year-old student from Kansas offers a good example of what can happen when neither person has had any experience or education: "My boyfriend of one year and I were both virgins, curious about sex, but totally clueless. At least we knew that the penis went into the vagina. Fortunately I was smart enough to be worried about pregnancy.

"The actual event was incredibly unpleasant. Who said it's supposed to be pleasurable, I thought! I knew he loved me, but I didn't know a thing about my body. I cried often afterward and felt miserable; my boyfriend didn't understand my reaction and we stopped attempting intercourse. I think that if I had known some basic things about my body, I might not have felt so degraded. Regardless of whether or not I had received any sex education, I would have been tempted to have intercourse at that time. In retrospect, I think I may have been modest and insecure about sex because when I was younger my babysitter's husband sexually abused me. It gave me mixed messages."

So many of these women talked about their own inexperience and felt embarrassed by their awkwardness and naivete. But like any skill or physical endeavor we try for the first time, we learn as we go. Just like the first time we ride a bike, we don't have our balance, the first time we make love, most of us do not know just how our body is going to respond; we have not yet discovered the fine tuning and balance of our own physical mechanisms. A young, white student from Illinois describes that learning process.

"The whole experience was sort of surreal. Both of us had been drinking, but not too much—neither of us was drunk. My memory of this experience isn't too terrific. I don't remember having any physical sensations of pleasure. I guess I was too scared that it would hurt. It didn't really, and we did use a condom for birth control.

Neither of us thought much about disease; AIDS was still considered a 'gay' disease, especially in Illinois. Mostly, it was a purely physical experience, very non-emotional with little foreplay or talking.

"In the past year I have met a man who has played a pivotal role in my sexual development. I think this comes from a combination of two things: love and honesty. I am very much in love with this man and our emotional ties get stronger, our sex lives get better. He is very honest and frank about what he would like sexually. He makes feel and has taught me to be just as open. Before, when I was was having sex, I was never able to say, 'Do this.' But now, with my fiance, I feel completely comfortable describing my needs. I have learned that if you want someone to satisfy you, you have to teach them how."

"It wasn't a particularly satisfying experience, and I was also incredibly naive," remembers a cook from Wisconsin, whose first time was while a college freshman. "I remember saying to him, when he came, that I could feel his heart beating. As I began to become more familiar with my body's responses to him, sex became a pleasurable experience, but the pleasure I felt during this time was not from an orgasm, but just from the fact of doing 'it.' It seems to have been an indication of a boundary crossing into a more committed relationship."

"It is a wise virgin who looks after her own lamp."
—*Jennie Jerome Churchill, "Bystander"*

As the woman above notes, as time goes on and women become more comfortable with their bodies—and the more they practice—physical intimacy gets better, as this Jewish college professor in her early thirties details: "My first experience was planned with my boyfriend of one year. In fact, it was so planned that I had already been to a gynecologist and was ready with my birth-control method, a diaphragm.

"I did not feel pressured. In fact, I was more than ready. During the act itself, I was anxious (all of those expectations...), which doesn't make for the most enjoyable sex! Afterward, I felt somewhat let down. It did get much better as time went on.

"The turning point in my sexuality came in graduate school with a man with whom I was friends. I was quite sexually attracted to him, although in a more subdued way than the men I had dated in the past. Once we began sleeping together, I discovered a whole new world. My first boyfriend and I had been sexually compatible, but comfortable, almost complacent. This man was exciting and fantastic. We had the best sex over the following year and a half."

Many young women expect that the male will take the lead and know how to give them pleasure without their knowing anything about their own bodies. "I had waited a long time for the right person to come along, and when I was twenty-two, he finally did," said a twenty-three-year-old salesperson from California. "I secretly went on the pill and, after waiting several months and enjoying the security of us being together, I decided it was time.

"We were having one of our heavy-petting sessions and, before we reached the actual stage where we usually stopped I asked him if we were going to 'do it.' I pulled out a condom (I was worried about disease, because I knew he had slept with other women), but it didn't work (nerves and all). "Then he said that he'd never been a fan of condoms anyway. Of course, I translated that to mean that he never used condoms with his partners and concluded that he must have AIDS. I quickly rationalized, probably stupidly, that odds were he didn't have AIDS and that it would be okay to have unprotected sex. We tried again to do it, but it didn't work. I was dry, and he couldn't come; our bodies were telling us what we couldn't verbalize. Naturally, I was disappointed because I had waited so long. I felt like he should have tried harder to make me excited; I wanted him to take on more of a teaching role, but he did not want that, as he later told me. We both apologized and fell asleep—unsatisfied, but knowing it could only get better. He didn't tell me he loved me that night, which really made me wonder if I had made the right decision."

In several cases, good experiences were the result of the sensitivity and experience of the woman's partner.

Often older men, who had more experience and were communicative, enjoyed taking the lead and created a loving environment for a woman's first time. Says a sixty-one-year-old white psychotherapist from Michigan, "We made a great special occasion out of it: Went first to a hotel and signed in as 'Mr. and Mrs.' We'd been planning it for weeks. He was sexually more experienced than I, and also older. He treated me with gentleness and respect. I felt safe and tenderly cared for and never regretted a thing."

Even if the partner had no experience, sensitivity played an even more important role, as this twenty-year-old Catholic from Illinois explained: "Homecoming weekend of my senior year in high school seemed to be the perfect time to consummate my relationship with my boyfriend of three months. Not so coincidentally, I got sick and postponed the event until the following week. The most significant aspect was simply getting it over with, getting past the discomfort. My boyfriend, also a virgin, was consistently loving if not extremely nervous, like myself.

"At the time, I felt confused about my sexuality as a result of earlier experiences. I really mistrusted boys in general because I had been constantly touched without my consent and forced into compromising situations while growing up. Because I had large breasts at an early age, boys assumed it meant I was easy. This was hardly the case, and I continually felt degraded and blamed myself for boys shoving me in closets, pushing their hands up my shirt, and tackling me in the schoolyard. When my boyfriend started fondling my breasts one time, I started to cry, feeling scared that he would hurt me and tell me I was a slut like the boys had done before.

"The only grasp I had of sex was that it would always be negative. Even when a nice, caring guy came along, the bad experiences prohibited me from letting go and trusting. I had to heal a lot, and luckily my first time was a stepping stone in reforming and redefining myself. I sensed a glimmer of possibility that I could learn to trust someone with my body and feel comfortable with myself as a sexual person. Fortunately, I chose an understanding and compassionate partner as my first lover."

A thirty-two-year-old restaurant manager also had a loving and sensitive partner. "I had been close friends for a year or so with Peter, and although we never discussed sex, we knew we were both waiting for the right time. We planned a holiday together at a bed-and-breakfast, and I went on the pill. I remember being very ill at ease during the preparations for bed and feeling very self-conscious about my nudity. Peter was a sweet guy and kept asking me if it hurt (he was equipped like a stallion—the largest I have ever experienced—which was a bit rough for the first time). I loved feeling physically close to someone. I grew up in a family that didn't touch or show affection; I was always the odd one out in that regard. The day after our first time, I remember smiling a lot and cuddling as we walked, hand in hand, around the farm. It was all very innocent and natural."

One thirty-seven-year-old business manager from Missouri waited for all of the right elements—birth control planning, sensitivity, communication, and willingness to learn and teach—before she decided to have sex. The results were wonderful, as she remembers. "When I began dating, I dated some really nice boys and was never in danger or felt out of control. The farthest I went without penetration was getting into bed with one of my boyfriends without our clothes on. My body delighted in the skin contact.

"Finally, when I did go all the way it was on New Year's Eve in my brother's bed in the apartment over my parent's garage. I was a senior in high school and had been dating my boyfriend for about three months—he was my first true love and we stayed together for two years. I was happy that I had waited to experience sex with someone I was in love with and trusted fully. He was not a virgin, but had been very patient with me. The lovemaking was pretty well planned: I went on the pill beforehand because most of my friends had been on it for a while and were sexually active.

"When it was over, I was curious about why losing your virginity was considered such a big deal—I mean, there was no blood, no pain; all I felt was that he was still in me even after he wasn't. Maybe a few years of tampons destroyed my hymen; maybe I never had one.

"Since there was no real physical passage for me to go through, my loss of virginity served as a doorway to my growth and maturity as an adult. Looking back, I remember telling myself that I had crossed the threshold into womanhood, that I 'was a woman now.'

"Later, during the sixties and seventies, I went through periods of what I would now consider promiscuity, prior to my marriage and after my divorce (the first man I had an orgasm with was my husband, after teaching myself through masturbating in college). I experimented quite a bit but never with women. I am quite enough woman for myself, and although I admire women for their strength and beauty, a sexual relationship would be too many breasts and vaginas in one bed, too much womanness for me. I understand now that I was seeking affirmation, not sexual gratification with all that experimentation. Now I affirm and gratify myself, until or unless a mature, promising relationship develops.

"Part of this re-evaluation of my sexuality occurred because I contracted genital herpes from the first man I dated after my divorce. This has had an impact on my whole identity—not only on my self-esteem and feeling of wholeness as a woman, but on the vulnerability of my health. Revealing this to potential lovers has had mixed results—from a man who quickly terminated the relationship to a man who said, 'Oh, that's too bad, let's make love.' Regardless, I try not to take risks anymore."

As these stories graphically demonstrate, planning for the event is just one of the elements that comprise a positive first experience. Planning empowers women to enter into sex without fear of pregnancy or disease and with a feeling of control; but logistical planning alone cannot prepare a young woman for the vast physical and emotional terrain that opens up with sexual intimacy.

Nonetheless, these women are groundbreakers. Many other women felt guilt for being sexual or felt that the choice wasn't really theirs to make. And there are also young women who feel that being a virgin is a social stigma, something to remedy.

Where we find ourselves on the spectrum is a result of a confluence of factors, notes Lillian Rubin. "Whatever else we may say about sex," she writes in *Erotic Wars*, "it is at least as much a social and psychological phenomenon as it is a biological one. Even the gender differences in sexuality are profoundly influenced by the commandments and constraints of the culture . . . Thus, whether we accept the sexual restrictions of our age, struggle against them, or vacillate somewhere between the two, the context is defined by the historical moment through which we are passing."

Just Get it Over With

"I lay, rapt and naked, on Irwin's ruffled blanket, waiting for the miraculous change to make itself felt. But all I felt was a sharp, startling bad pain."

–Sylvia Plath

One of the female rites of passage, among such others as menstruation, pregnancy, childbirth, and menopause, is defloration, an event that many women want simply to get over with. Not all women believe that their hymen, their virginity, is something that should be taken to the marriage bed or saved for "the man they love." Quite the opposite is sometimes true: Many women want to have some experience before falling in love, knowing that the first time can be awkward, painful, and even humiliating. "Why have this experience with someone you love?" these women remarked.

Unlike the planners, women who fell into this category generally expected their first time to be a negative experience, a necessary prelude to the blossoming of their full sexuality. "I wanted to get the painful part over with with someone I didn't care about, so that when I did fall in love, I wouldn't be so scared and anxious," said one woman. Commented another, "I don't think that the sharing of your virginity is necessarily a gift to a man—I mean, it can be a miserable experience."

This perspective of the first time being an ordeal for

women is not unrealistic. According to Daniel Evan
Weiss in *The Great Divide*, 59 percent of women surveyed didn't enjoy the experience whereas only 14
percent of men didn't. A twenty-five-year-old chef
raised in Virginia tells a typical tale.

"I was a bitter and cynical teenager, worried about
global problems and hating the pettiness of my high
school peers. Having sex was just another experience of
growing up that I wanted to get over with. I don't think
I had seen enough movies, because I was very ignorant
of the actual mechanics. But I knew enough to go on the
pill and did so without the knowledge of my boyfriend.
One day, I allowed him to penetrate, much to his surprise; it wasn't a big deal because it hurt like hell and
wasn't fun at all. I think it was a convenient situation,
and I wanted to have a boyfriend and an experience.
After that, my sexuality slowly kicked in and I realized
that I was unfilled having loveless sex—it made me feel
hollow. Still, I felt mature, but it took a while for it all to
come together (no pun intended)."

Many of the women who fall into the "just get it over
with" category are from the post-women's movement
generation, part of the transitional phase of changing
sexual attitudes. Suddenly, almost overnight, the rules
changed. As Lillian Rubin says in *Erotic Wars*, "[I]n the
brief span of one generation—from the 1940s to the
1960s—we went from mothers who believed their vir-

ginity was their most prized possession to daughters for whom it was a burden."

This created new pressures. "Certainly some women in the Movement felt sexually exploited rather than liberated by the sexual revolution, which they claimed created a new compulsory sex ethic," says Alice Echols in *Daring to Be Bad*. Many of the getting-it-over-with stories seem to come from this place—that women wanted to get past this hurdle, this social burden, so that they could begin the discovery of their sexual identity.

Here's a story from a forty-two-year-old accountant from South Carolina who literally went on a mission to lose her virginity. She, too, did not enjoy her first time— or many times thereafter. "I didn't learn the facts of life until I was eighteen, and even then I was covering my ears. Before that, I was afraid that you could get pregnant by dancing close, since it made me feel so hot. So it wasn't until I was twenty-one, when I was with one of my more adventurous friends, that I lost my virginity. She and I were at a bar where we met two men. Many beers later, we split up, each going to the home of our respective man. Mine was pretty drunk; I guess I felt safer with a stranger who was only half-conscious. I was not drunk. It wasn't memorable, he pulled out before ejaculation, which turned out to be my method of birth control until I got pregnant two years later. I didn't ever enjoy sex until I had a steady boyfriend at age twenty-three. Even then I had a lot of guilt and felt inhibited—

mostly because I felt very self-conscious about my body. My enjoyment wasn't free and liberated, but rather surprising and passive. I frequently felt bored and impatient to get it over with. Sometimes I turned to drugs and alcohol to enhance my relaxation and enjoyment.

"Overall, my virginity meant a lot to me before I lost it and very little afterwards. It's certainly an overrated quality. Upon losing it, I may have felt a little proud— like I had arrived, become a woman. But it was by no means a watershed, except that I felt it was wrong and continued to struggle with my mother's values versus those of the 'love generation.'"

Some women didn't purposefully look for the experience, but took advantage of a spontaneous opportunity once it presented itself. "It kind of just happened," one woman stated, "and I thought, well, it might as well be now." The "get-it-over-with" aspect of the experience is summed up neatly by this thirty-year-old white lawyer, complete with a residue of guilt: "When I graduated from high school, I didn't want to go off to college a virgin. So on a Hawaiian vacation, I decided to do it with a guy I met during the week. We parted, I wrote to him, he never wrote back.

"Being raised a Catholic, I had certain guilt feelings about sex. It took me a long time (four or five) years to ever have an orgasm, and, of course, masturbation was out! But once I started being more comfortable with myself and masturbating, I realized that I could make sex work for me and my partner.

"My mother still thinks I was almost a virgin until I got married this year."

There's often a very dissociated sense to the stories of these women, as though their bodies belonged to someone else and were simply passive vehicles used to mark the steps to adulthood. Here's a twenty-one-year-old California student's description: "I didn't really know the guy. He was in a class I was taking outside of high school and was four or five years older. He asked me to his house for a movie, and I knew that if I said yes, I would have to have sex. That was okay with me. I wanted to get this part of growing up over with, and I didn't see myself as having the chance again. I didn't want to do it the first time awkwardly with someone I really cared about—or so I had convinced myself. The whole experience hurt and bored me. We were on the floor in front of the couch and my head was turned away. The movie *Gremlins* was playing, and I just kept watching the television.

"I've never been in love nor had an orgasm. My body seems to have just not gotten there yet. I guess I cannot give up my self-control until I care about someone enough."

"Close your eyes and think of England."
       —Queen Victoria's sexual advice to her daughter

Some women didn't communicate to their partner that it was their first time; hence they felt that the discomfort and awkwardness could have been alleviated with more communication. Often, the information was withheld because of embarrassment over inexperience and ignorance. "On Valentine's Day at age fifteen," writes a twenty-one-year-old white Episcopalian, "my boyfriend and I began kissing and fondling each other— no pressure to have sex was there. I was very relaxed and it all seemed very gentle and slow. I wasn't worried about disease, birth control, or pain; the only thought I had was: Who did my boyfriend have sex with prior to dating me? The next evening I realized that he hadn't really penetrated me, because we did it again and I bled all over the sheets and it did hurt this time. I was embarrassed about the situation and not able to talk with him about it. Because I felt so humiliated about the blood, I became very modest with my first partner."

Some women, although seeking the experience, afterward felt as though they have truly lost something, like this thirty-one-year-old Jewish woman raised in New York: "I lost my virginity in a rose garden in the Blue Ridge Mountains. Though it sounds rather romantic, it really wasn't. My body was mature at fifteen, my hormones racing, my curiosity piqued, but my spirit wasn't ready for it. I was dating a boy, two years my senior, during a summer of volunteer work in Virginia. Knowing I was far away from my parents, I guess I knew that sex with him was inevitable. In fact, I was much more curious about the experience than the person. After it was over, I cried. I knew something was irrevocably lost—much more than just my intact hymen. I no longer completely belonged to myself; I had given something away rather than shared it, and that made me very sad.

"It took several years before I had an inkling of what sexual sharing was. It was not until I fell in love in college that I began waking up and reveling in any kind of bodily sensations. Sex can be either incredibly alienating or connecting. I began to understand the possibility for connection when sex and love are together; it was with the first man I had an orgasm with and the entire experience was very powerful.

"Only in the past few years have I gained a sense of power from sex, mostly because I'm becoming stronger and more independent. I believe that sex is never distant from where you are spiritually, although I certainly had some highly charged experiences when I was younger. It is only now that I leave lovemaking intact; it no longer takes something away from me, because I am no longer giving it away. Rather, I'm learning what it means to share. I am learning only now what it means to recognize and honor my own strengths."

In contrast to those who felt guilt or sadness over losing their virginity, some women were ashamed to be labeled a virgin, equating it with naivete and lack of sophistication. For these women, defloration was the entry to adulthood, as Molly Ivins, in *Molly Ivins Can't Say That Can She?*, comments: "Back when I went to college, listening to Dave Brubeck and Edith Piaf was a fundamental prerequisite for sophistication, on a par with losing your virginity." For a thirty-eight-year-old Jewish secretary from New York this was definitely true. "I had a tremendous crush on this guy in college and wanted to do it. He didn't want to have to deal with a virgin, so I told him I wasn't one. It felt like rebellion and one of the first conscious adult choices I had made. Up until then, I hadn't even French kissed much, but I felt that now I wanted to have the experience. I went to Planned Parenthood as a way of acting responsibly and to pretend I was physically ready. I remember the whole time feeling tight and scared and trying to hide, in what felt like an incredibly embarrassing and clumsy way, that I was a virgin. I had convinced myself that I was in love and wanted to do this with him. Afterward, after no physical sensation or pleasure, he began to kind of back-step, suddenly telling me about some other girl he met. That felt horrible.

"The only purpose this experience served was really to just get it over with. It paved the way for me to get on with my sexuality and be more selective. The second man I slept with was older, and I actually had an incredible time. We had a pitcher of beer together, he said the classic, 'Wanna come over to my place?' I got there and he had a waterbed, sexy music on the stereo, and I was thinking, 'Wow, this is good; I can dig this.' I hadn't realized that I had so much control over my own orgasm during sex, but this guy knew what he was doing also. I had a slight revelation, 'So this is what they're talking about.' It was a purely physical, sexual kind of thing."

For those who did want to get it over with, the need to feel mature or gain experience was not always the prime motivator. Sometimes, as this thirty-seven-year-old Chicano health administrator relates, the onset of their sexuality piqued their curiosity and led them to explore. She was lucky and had a wonderful first experience. "I was very embarrassed and tired of wearing the label 'virgin.' I felt like I was the oldest virgin in the world and being a virgin meant I was undesirable, unattractive, and even asexual. So, at age nineteen, I secretly planned to lose it at the first safe opportunity.

"When a man I knew, who was a friend of a friend of a friend, started to show some interest in me, I decided to go home with him. This was pretty out of character for me; I was painfully shy and really wanted to meet someone, fall in love, and be swept away. But my patience had run out and so with a faked bravado (I always tried to pass off my shyness and naivete as toughness; looking back I doubt it worked), I went to his place. Previously, my only experience was kissing a boy

---

"Virginity is rather a state of mind."
    —Maxwell Anderson, "Elizabeth the Queen"

in high school. However, to my body's relief, I had just discovered masturbation a few months earlier. " T h e guy I was with was twenty-five and had been around the block—although I'm sure he knew I was new at this. We smoked some strong pot, and I was glad to be a little stoned; it made me feel loose and giggly and more uninhibited sexually. He was actually, I see in retrospect, a pretty considerate lover. Pure luck. I could have so easily been with someone who didn't care about how I was doing—or worse! Anyway, we were smoking pot on his bed, and lay back and began kissing. Immediately I was very excited, but he proceeded slowly: undressing me, kissing me, and sucking my breasts and stomach. Then he even used a rubber (without any discussion!). It wasn't until many years later that I realized how lucky I was. Anyway, we went on to have intercourse and I had a wonderful orgasm.

"Later we were lying on the bed and one of his roommates burst in—presumably to get the pot. I was more preoccupied with being embarrassed at being seen naked and in a blatant post-coital state. When the roommate left, I jumped out of bed and began getting dressed. The man I was with apologized and tried to convince me to stay, but I refused. The mood—if there had been one—was broken. I'd accomplished my goal and wanted to go back to my life. I never saw him again. He called me, and I talked with him once and made an excuse for not seeing him again. He asked if it was because of the sex, and I said, 'Oh no, it was wonderful.'

Poor guy, I'm sure he felt thoroughly confused.

"I didn't have sex again for another year, but I definitely felt more power and control from the experience. I did feel suddenly awakened, although that was probably related to starting to masturbate. (One day I just decided to insert some pseudo-dildo object into my vagina, as I had read about, and try to get off. And I did! Before that, I barely touched myself 'down there'; I had never even inserted a tampon before.) My first encounter had confirmed that I was a healthy, attractive sexual being. It also foreshadowed future sexual relations because I've always felt in control and have always had orgasms."

Several women who came of age in the sixties and early seventies felt that losing their virginity was a political statement, an emancipation of the most rebellious and personal kind. "At age eighteen as a freshman in college," relates a forty-four-year-old Jewish writer from Missouri, "I was involved with a boyfriend from my hometown who was attending a different college. Though we were boyfriend and girlfriend, I wouldn't say we were in love, and the question of marriage certainly never arose between us. But I was eager to lose my virginity. It was the '60s, and it seemed like the thing to do—more coming from an idea than from my body. I didn't feel pressured by him so much as by the wonderful idea of sex, which at the time meant some kind of liberation.

"He came to visit for a weekend and we went to a rather run-down hotel together and (very anticlimactically) had sex. Because of wanting to avoid pregnancy, we used the withdrawal method (really Russian Roulette) and he pulled out before he came. It was quick and not particularly satisfying or pleasurable for me. After he came, he said, 'Well, that's it,' and I thought, That's it? (I had been masturbating since age eleven or twelve and knew what it meant to have an orgasm!) I felt lonely and disappointed; he didn't speak to me or touch me lovingly in any way. I broke off our relationship shortly thereafter, went on the Pill and then on a sexual spree—many partners, some one-night stands, some sexual encounters with women. To an outsider it would appear that sex was important to me, though it was not all that pleasurable.

"I had my first orgasm during coitus when I was twenty-four, with the man to whom I have now been married for twenty years. And this, I must say, has been the only, truly satisfying sexual relationship I have had."

The function of sex as a form of rebellion for young women seemed to be part of the very normal process of finding themselves and discovering their needs. It also could mean liberation from parental values, as this forty-year-old artist from California reveals: "The first week away at college I lost my virginity with the help of a young man I had just met. After we were introduced,

I went to the university health center, stood in line for several hours, feeling like a herded cow, and was examined by an insensitive male physician to receive birth-control pills. I then had sex with the fellow. (This is a good example of how little I knew—birth-control pills don't offer protection until a month after you begin taking them.)

"Kissing and fondling were much more exciting than the penetration. Mostly, I was relieved to have experienced 'the act.' I remember feeling a combination of guilt and power and independence. I was angry and rebellious my first semester of college in a way that I had never been at home. One way I rebelled was that my first boyfriend was not Jewish, and I was ashamed and angry at my parents because I knew they would find him objectionable. In fact, I refuse to talk to my parents for three months—exactly the length of time the relationship lasted.

"I didn't experience orgasm with a partner until three years later, although I'd been masturbating to orgasm since I was a child. At the community center swimming pool as a kid, I somehow figured out that if I placed myself at a certain angle to the water jets, I could give myself an orgasm. Of course, I didn't know exactly what was happening until I was about sixteen. I never let anyone know what I was doing; it was a secret I never shared.

"My last semester of college I went to study in Hong Kong. The sex I had there was the wildest physically that I have ever had. It was the first time I had an orgasm with a partner and the first and last time I put myself in a dangerous situation. One night, when it was too late to get home by ferry, I spent the night with a man whom I felt slightly nervous about. I didn't want to have sex with him; I wasn't on the pill and condoms weren't around. He entered me anally several times which I found painful and humiliating because it was against my will. I never acted so stupidly as I did that night, and it took more than ten years before I could enjoy sex with anal penetration."

Secretly doing something you know your parents wouldn't approve of is silent defiance. But here's a woman who flagrantly defied her parents—with family threats as a consequence:

"I had two experiences I consider to be my initiation," remembers a twenty-five-year-old Catholic teacher. "The first was at age fifteen with a boy I had known for several years. He lived in a small country town and was very close to my cousin and her husband. I would go up there quite often, and eventually the boy and I developed a crush on each other. One evening, when we were baby-sitting my little cousin, we began to mess around. This was probably the third or fourth time we had been physical. Things progressed and we were partially naked. He put his penis inside of me, only for a few minutes, and pulled out before he came. We were both afraid that my cousin would come home. He soon left and we never really discussed it after that night. I think that we were both in shock that we had done it.

"The second experience, which occurred about six or seven months later, is what I really consider 'losing my virginity.' I had been going out with a guy for about eight months. I really liked him even though we were very different. He was a high school senior; I was a freshman. He was black; I was white. The small town we lived in was almost purely white and needless to say, quite a few heads turned, including my father's—which for the most part is why I held on to the relationship for so long. When my father found out we were seeing each other, he forbade me to see him. I told my father he was a racist, but he claimed that my boyfriend's color had nothing to do with it—he was just too old for me. So we did what we had to do to see each other, which meant sneaking around a lot. One night when my parents were out, we met in my family's guest house. On that night, for some reason, we both decided to have sex. Afterward, I was confused by the whole thing; it wasn't what I had imagined—it was kind of boring. I still felt relieved that it was over with. After he left I went and sat on the toilet, hoping that all of his semen would fall out.

"My first sexual experiences are very important to me, but I have never thought of them as wonderful or enjoyable. Over time, as I have become clearer about who I am, I have arrived at another level of

---

Some Hindu sects require a priest to deflower a virgin before she consummates the marriage with her husband.

experiencing my sexuality. I really enjoy sex now and feel at home in my body when I am sexual, whether it is with myself or with a man I love."

Sadly, some women felt that when growing up, the only way they could receive affection was through physical contact, searching for emotional connection through sex. Eventually these women realized that they first needed emotional intimacy in order to have physical satisfaction, not vice versa. But it was a learning process to realize what they needed. A nurse from New York exemplifies this.

"After breaking up with my first boyfriend, I felt so sad I didn't care what I did. I just wanted to get it over with. I was a heavy drinker and into drugs and used these chemicals to cope with my feelings. I would go to bars (I was eighteen, which was the drinking age in New York), get smashed, and pick up guys. Once, when I was on vacation in Florida, I went wild, picked up a few guys, and had intercourse with them, unplanned, no birth control, while drinking. I got in many situations where I was drunk and didn't know the guy and could have been raped. I was fortunate that this never happened (at least I have no memory of it, although blacking out was a regular occurrence) or that I never got pregnant or caught any sexually transmitted diseases. I also had sex with guys that I had had friendships with, hoping that some kind of emotional connection would develop. I was always disappointed. It seemed that no guys could love me for who I was, unconditionally, like I was willing to love them. And I felt the physical was overrated and ho-hum.

"So, the specific act of 'losing my virginity' seems to be one big blur. Looking back on this time, I realize how messed up I was and how desperately I wanted someone to talk to. Now I'm thirty-five, don't drink or use drugs anymore, and have been married for eight years to a man who is loving and intimate. For me, the key to sex is emotional intimacy; this seems to go hand-in-hand with feeling sexually satisfied.

"It's too bad there was no one there to help me with this struggle at a critical time when the physical act of intercourse was emphasized as the great experience. (My mother was a victim of sexual abuse and an alcoholic who tried but was obviously not fit.) Answering these questions has stirred up my past history and emotions I haven't thought about for a long time. I've learned about myself by helping you with your book. Thank you for allowing me to participate. It was a turbulent time; I'm glad I'm not eighteen again."

As the previous story illustrates, a great number of the "get it-over-with" stories involve drugs or alcohol: alcohol lessened the inhibitions and even the pain many women felt; it gave them the courage (or numbness) to just go out and do it, with no regard to their true wants, morals, or needs. A thirty-two-year-old white heroin addict tells her story: "I lost my virginity when I was sixteen. It was pretty average. I was a little drunk. It was awkward and it was a relief to get it over with. It didn't matter in my life in the big picture; in fact, it seems like kind of a joke to even tell you about it. I mean, now I've got four kids (I never was good with birth control), who live with foster families. I have visiting rights some- times—mostly I call them on the telephone on their birthdays. I've traded sex a lot for dope. It's the only thing I have left that's supposedly worth something on the streets anymore. Nothing seems very real to me."

A waitress from Nebraska offers another example of the effects of combining drugs and alcohol with sex. "My friend and I planned to lose our virginity at the same time—actually who could lose it first. We were living together in a foster home and decided to run away to Omaha, Nebraska, to both have sex for the first time. We were under the influence of drugs and alcohol. I slept with her boyfriend's brother—it hurt like hell and I bled all over the sheets. Before this, I was very naive about sex. Guys and sometimes even my foster brothers were always trying to force me to have sex with them from about seventh grade on, but I always managed to keep them off of me. After I lost my virginity, though, I

"Virginity breeds mites, much like a cheese consumes itself to the very paring, and so it dies with feeding its own stomach. Besides virginity is peevish, proud, idle, made of self-love, which is the most inhibited sin in the canon."
—William Shakespeare, "All's Well that Ends Well"

began to give in a lot, always because of alcohol.

"Now I don't drink, and sex is great. In fact, I've been with the same guy for ten years and he has never forced me. We didn't even have sex the first three times because he couldn't. Wow, what a difference. He really brought me out sexually; I became more open and aggressive, asking and showing and even talking about my needs. Also, when we both slept with another woman, it added a new dimension to our sex life."

This twenty-five-year-old's partner was so drunk he didn't even remember having sex with her: "As a late-blooming, tomboyish teen, I felt like my ship had finally come in when I was a sophomore in high school. Boys my age, who had ruthlessly teased me for years, were suddenly inconsequential as upperclassmen began to give me attention. I began dating a senior. Not only was he older, but he was quarterback of the football team, good-looking, and on his way to an Ivy League college. At age sixteen, I was amazed that he had noticed me, but also felt that I finally was being noticed for me! I was in love—puppy love, that first intense, crush kind of love, hormones-racing love. Up until then, my previous sexual experience included the usual groping, awkward make-out sessions. My body seemed to me like a foreign land, and I was certain that my bony hips and small breasts were utterly unattractive.

"One night, after some very serious drinking, we ended up at my house; he snuck in my bedroom window with my parents fast asleep down the hall. Just seconds before, I had heard him throwing up in my backyard. But suddenly he was in my bed, and in a drunken, dulled passion, we were 'doing it.' I remember thinking to myself, Well, this is it. I'm having sex now, his penis is inside of me. The physical sensation didn't hurt much, probably because I was so drunk, but it felt like trying to force something in a place that it didn't really fit—like your thumb up your nose. We didn't talk about it, or that I was a virgin (he wasn't) until about six months later. Not surprisingly, he didn't even remember that night as our first time; he remembered our second time, which was much more romantic and tender. Although he tried, I could never orgasm with him—or myself for that matter—and always felt inadequate, inexperienced, and painfully self-conscious.

"Several months after our relationship ended, I had the most spectacular wet dream. I woke up to an orgasm and felt like a wave of technicolor lust was rushing through my body, originating from places that had seemed like frontier until then. I was thrilled that my body worked and began to masturbate regularly— what a revelation! In this way, I was much more prepared for my next lover. I could help him understand the road map to my body, because now I knew it myself. Of course, I was terrified that no other person could make me come, only I could please myself. So, it was with gratefulness and relief that I had my first orgasm with a man. It was a switch having a man want to really please me and able to communicate with me about it. It was also such a switch to feel sexy and desirable; I knew that I was loved. The first time I had an orgasm with my sweetheart, through manual stimulation, I remember looking at the ceiling and thinking: Yes, this is how it's supposed to be—giving and receiving; this is it. It was heavenly."

Sometimes alcohol aided women in deluding themselves, making them feel as though they were ready for sex, as this forty-six-year-old realtor from Texas relates: "Sexual involvement to me was supposed to be the springboard to marriage. So when I lost my virginity my freshman year in college to a boy I had been dating for four months, I deemed it acceptable because I assumed he would be 'the one.' He invited me out of town for the weekend. I didn't plan it and didn't even give a fleeting thought to birth control. We were experimenting with alcohol (which was the early stage of my alcoholism) and the temporary lack of inhibitions that the alcoholic buzz gave me created a false sense of emotional maturity, as though I was ready for the next step in life.

"Physically, I think my body was ready for the experience; I actually don't remember any pain. Emotionally, though, it was the beginning of a long pattern of avoiding my emotions with alcohol. I had come from a dysfunctional, alcoholic family and the lack of communication in my family set a bad precedent that took me years to unlearn. There was also an uncle who fondled me when I was five, maybe six. At the time, I had sensed that it wasn't right, but I was in my late twenties before I began addressing the issue.

"After my first experience, I realized the control, or what I thought was control, that sex gave me. I continued deluding myself in this mode until my sixth year of sobriety at age forty-five. It took a failed marriage and love affair to make me realize I could not continue the same behavior expecting different results. I have now stopped being sexually active, am dating a variety of men, and am experiencing intimacy without sex. I am excited to finally realize that respect is what I always wanted and not control, which I mistook as power over my own life."

This thirty-four-year-old editor from Pennsylvania sums up a lot of the themes of this chapter: embarrassment over being a virgin, lack of communication with her partner, and wishing for more sex education. She also expresses the desire that the experience be different for her daughters and offers a perspective on how it can be. "I lost my virginity when I was working at an amusement park in Ohio. I was eighteen and a half and embarrassed that I had completed my entire freshman year in college without taking the plunge.

"My roommates were both seniors, and when they asked me if I was a virgin, I answered, 'Well, kind of.' Needless to say that warranted a big laugh and lots of teasing. What I had meant was that I had been in some sexual situations, but had yet to have intercourse.

"Anyway, I was eager to be initiated and my first experience was memorable, if not good. I did not tell the fellow, who was about two years older than me, that it was my first time. I now regret that. Had I been wise, I would have dished it up on a silver platter and received the sympathy, tenderness, and respect that anyone embarking on their first act of intercourse deserves.

"We went out on a date to a bar, got exceedingly drunk, and somehow ended up on a small power boat docked at a marina. It was about as romantic as the backseat of a car. We were under the cabin section on a vinyl benchlike seat. I was so terrified, I didn't move during the entire event or for the rest of the night. In the morning my back was stuck to the vinyl, and I practically pulled my skin off when I tried to get up.

"My date's romantic comment to me after the event was: 'Boy, was I horny. Weren't you?' Maybe that's one reason I regret not telling him. There was such a huge communication gap. He had no idea how I felt, because I was hiding everything. I was so confused as to what I was supposed to be like. After growing up in a conservative Catholic family, it's difficult to jump off the sexual ledge and go from total repression to red-hot mama.

"When he dropped me off at the employee dorm the next morning, I felt a massive amount of liquid dripping between my legs. Trying to walk as fast as I could with my legs together, I scurried toward the door, praying he wasn't watching me. When I got inside, I found my jeans thoroughly soaked—I looked like I wet my pants. All I can imagine was that he was certainly telling the truth about being horny and had had a huge backlog of sperm. Nothing like that ever occurred on our few times together afterward, and I've never experienced anything like that since.

"Even though the experience was bad, I felt worldly, womanly and cool. Looking back, I see that it paved the way for several years' worth of terrible sexual experiences. In fact, although I had one orgasm in high school, I didn't have another one until I graduated from college. During this time, foolishly I never masturbated. For starters, I didn't know how to, and I actually thought that only disgusting, pathetic, desperate people did that sort of thing. I was a typically repressed, mixed-up young woman. There's so much I regret about my sexual past. If only I could go back with the experience and confidence I have now, I feel like I could take over the world.

"In thinking back about my sexuality, I can pinpoint a lot of problems. The most obvious is a lack of sex education. I literally had none except for a menstruation booklet and film. The second negative was the double standard imposed on girls—which we're all so familiar with—that it's okay and natural for boys to have and

---

"Such a one as cannot keep her maidenhood will never keep a secret."

—Deloney, *"The Gentle Craft"*

explore sexual feelings, but not for girls.

"I want to give my daughters as much information on sex as I possibly can. I would also stress that they need to feel comfortable with someone, to trust him, if they're going to enjoy the experience. And if they aren't enjoying it, they should stop and ask themselves, 'why am I doing this?'"

Violation
in All Its Forms

"When they say the word 'taboo' I try to catch their eye. Are they saying something is 'sacred' and therefore not to be publicly examined for fear of disturbing the mystery; or are they saying it is so profane it must not be exposed, for fear of corrupting the young? Or are they saying simply that they can not and will not be bothered to listen to what is said about an accepted tradition of which they are a part . . ."

—Alice Walker,
Possessing the Secret of Joy

Just as there are many kinds of abuse, there are myriad violations, but what ties the women in this chapter together is that all had sexual choice taken away from them. Some were molested or raped as children; others experienced date rape as teens or young adults. (Although some women who answered the questionnaire had been raped by a stranger in their lifetime, none reported stranger rape as their first experience.) In each case, nobody asked and therefore nobody consented.

Childhood Sexual Abuse

As Susan Brownmiller points out in *Against Our Will: Men, Women and Rape*, while "the routine occurrence of child molestation remains a subject from which people prefer to avert their eyes," the sad truth is that many women were sexually abused as children. The reported figures remain consistent. The *Kinsey Report on Sexual Behavior in the Human Female*, published in 1953, found that one in four women reported some sort of unwanted preadolescent sexual experience with an adult male. And in the *Janus Report*, published in 1993, 23 percent of the women surveyed said they had been molested as children (11 percent of men said yes). Of those, 62 percent reported that it was by a relative, 21 percent by a stranger, and 17 percent by a person in authority.

My findings, although statistically inconclusive, were remarkably similar. Of the women who responded, 24 percent reported being sexual abused as children, with slightly over half reporting that the perpetrator was a relative.

The women who reported such abuse were profoundly affected. Not just their sexuality, but their identity, their self-confidence level, and the values with which they used to measure themselves were all contorted to fit these scarring childhood experiences. It was as if they all were, as one woman commented, "looking in a broken mirror trying to find a clear picture" of themselves.

Several women who wrote were just remembering abuse. Often, as memories were regained, low self-esteem was explained. Fear of men, bitterness, resentment, and anger all tended to be locked inside as companions to the feelings of a betrayed childhood. But, as many of these women note, with their memories came the opportunity for resolution, healing, and growth.

The ceremonial rites of worship of the phallic god, Baalpeor, by the Moabites and Midianites, required circumcision of men, and the deflowering of young women by an artificial phallus.

A few women tell of being raped as children by relatives, their virginity taken from them by members of their own family. Here's a thirty-eight-year-old white Texan's story: "Answering these questions has been personally very therapeutic. If I had responded in my twenties, I would have bragged about how much fun it was to skip school at age sixteen, staying home to make love with my nineteen-year-old boyfriend all day. Our families were strict Southern Baptist; we didn't use drugs or alcohol. Unbeknownst to my mom, I went to Planned Parenthood and went on the Pill. Physically I was totally ready and loved the feeling of being loved. Afterward, I felt great . . . there's nothing in the world like that slow, breathy 'Don't . . . stop' foreplay!

"Soon after, my sexual encounters became more frequent—and with a number of partners. Recently, through years of self-analysis, therapy, and education, I realized that my early sexual exploitations were very primitive attempts to be loved. My mother married seven times; my childhood was filled with turmoil and rejection. And I was raped by my brother, five years my senior, as a child. About two years ago, I gradually realized that I could not grow anymore as a person until I brought this out of the closet. I honestly did not realize the depth of pain and insecurity this experience had caused me until I began dealing with it.

"I know this seems a common phenomenon lately— but it really did take place. Fortunately, I have another brother who also remembers the horrors and supports me. Because of my sexual abuse, I felt my only value was as a sexual provider. And I must tell you that all my dear girlfriends who experienced sexual abuse as children fight a lifetime battle to attain a healthy self-image. We all measure our entire self-worth by our sexuality.

"Only now, in my late thirties, do I feel confident and complete enough to have a relationship with a man without feeling the need to be a sexual creature. This passage to feeling secure as a woman has been hard and has taken a lot of work, and I feel like I am speaking for the majority of women regarding our inner self-image."

Women who have endured such violation often become substance abusers. An African-American woman in her late forties, now a substance abuse counselor, relates her horror story. "The term 'losing your virginity' seems like a joke to me, probably because mine was rudely interrupted when at age three my stepfather started putting his dick in my mouth. It continued until age seven, but I'm not sure if that's when it stopped because my memory has failed me from that point onward.

"I thought it was a dream for many years because it happened in the middle of the night. I'd wake up with a nosebleed, and he'd be there to take me to the bathroom, then I'd return to bed and go back to sleep.

"Actual penetration occurred at age thirteen; the man was thirty-five. I am not too clear as to the circumstances except to say that he treated me with such kindness and love, which I was yearning for, that I did whatever he wanted. This spurred a twisted jealousy in my stepfather and he killed my lover, because he himself was planning on seducing me. Now my mother is remarried to another child molester.

"When I told my mother that her man was trying to seduce me and molesting me, she responded that I was trying to steal him from her. This confused and humiliated me. I became a runaway and alcoholic at age fourteen. I would have sex with anyone, no women however, just men and boys. I got pregnant at fourteen and a half and went to live with my paternal grandfather who was a smuggler in Mexico. He had men working for him who would pay me to feel my breasts. I lost the baby, probably because my body was undernourished due to drinking.

"I am still working through all these years of bullshit."

As the experience of this thirty-eight-year-old black mother of nine children reveals, family patterns of sexual abuse exist, where generation after generation of children become victims: "I come from a family where [sexual abuse] is considered a normal experience—normal, but one you try to avoid. My momma was very cautious. She had six girls and three boys. When my stepdad would try to get us daughters into the bathroom with him when he was going to be taking a bath, she would come after him with a gun and scare the shit out of him. See, my momma had the same thing happen to her, so she did her best to protect us.

"But she couldn't take care of us kids herself, so we were sent to live at our aunt's house, my momma's sister, in Texas. Well, we had a bad uncle, that's for sure. He'd always be bothering me and my sisters. He even did it to my brother. He'd have an excuse, like he was real sick, couldn't make it upstairs and had to sleep on the couch in our bedroom. He'd make up any old excuse to sleep near the kids. He raped all of us, and we would just cross our fingers hoping that it wasn't our turn.

"Because our momma had protected us at home, we thought we could tell our aunt and that she would believe us and chase off that bad uncle. Instead, she took us on a drive, me and all my sisters, and let us out in the middle of nowhere. She beat us. Told us we were lying and to keep our mouths shut and not to go near no husband of hers.

"This was Texas, after all, where the women protected their men and would believe them before they'd ever believe us kids. And even if they knew we were telling the truth, they didn't want to know about it.

"Now, I listen to my children, what every child tells me. When they tell me something, I investigate. My oldest boy came to me and he wanted to kill a neighbor man who molested him when he was fourteen. So even

---

Young Lenge girls of East Africa were required to be deflowered by a phallus made of horn as part of their ceremonial puberty rights.

if you try to protect your kids, you never know what happens to your kids when they leave your sight."

Here's another example of a woman telling her mother about abuse when it happened: "One of the first significant sexual experiences happened to me when I was about five or six," notes the white thirty-five-year-old from Wisconsin. "I was almost orally raped by a male baby-sitter. He came into my bedroom after I was asleep and asked me if I wanted some candy. He pulled out his penis. I started crying and he got scared and left the room. He was probably worried that I would wake one of my brothers. I told my mother about it a few days later. Recently she told me it freaked her out incredibly—I understand, I would be too if someone did that to one of my children. My parents never confronted the boy or his parents, they were members of the same church, but they terminated all dealings with the entire family. The pediatrician my mother consulted said the best thing about the situation was that I had told her, and that apparently he did not force himself on me."

Unlike the previous stories where the women remembered reacting to their abuse and asking for help as children, some women who related these stories were in various stages of regaining memories of childhood sexual abuse. The following story, by a young, white secretary from California, poignantly depicts the profound effect such abuse can have on a woman's sexuality.

"I am currently remembering childhood sexual

abuse. I haven't remembered any specific event, but I know it happened at age seven and it was my maternal grandfather. I know too that it was traumatic enough to have made me extremely uncomfortable with men in any context. It also explains a great deal about my anxiety and avoidance of intimacy.

"Never having had sex with a man, I've never technically 'lost my virginity.' I had a lesbian affair for two years. We stopped having sex after five months; I never had an orgasm. I liked the closeness, the kissing and cuddling, but not the rest of it. I felt a little disgusted and humiliated if I was touched around my genitals. I could never relax. The woman I was involved with later started to remember her own sexual abuse. It was a non-relationship—we never connected mentally or sexually. I did find being with a woman a real turn-on, but that was a very early reaction, which faded after a short while.

"I've gone through stages when I felt I could live without sex—that idea was very appealing. Now, however, I feel much more restless sexually, much more willing to consider being with a woman or man eventually. I'm not sure how I feel about lesbian sex anymore—it still appeals, I guess. And even though the memories of abuse have been painful, I feel as though my sexuality has been returned to me."

Date Rape

"We must continue to question cultural beliefs that permit a double standard of sexual morality and then use that double standard to justify male mistreatment of women."

—Karen Johnson, M.D., *Trusting Ourselves*

For the first time in history, we have a word to describe women being forced to have sex with someone they know. We can call it "acquaintance rape" or "date rape," but it is still rape. It is forcing sex on a woman who does not consent, and includes having sex with someone who is so drunk that the concept of consent is meaningless.

Although society is finally recognizing date rape for what it is, the double standard is still alive and well. When I was in high school in the mid-eighties, a girl I knew went to a party and got so drunk that she passed out. In this state, seven or eight male classmates had sex with her. The next day, rumors flew—rumors castigating the girl for being promiscuous. I will never forget one of the boys, who had admitted to me that he had had sex with her, yelling out "Slut!" across the schoolyard as she walked past. This was a boy who had been on top of her just the night before. Needless to say, she chose to transfer schools.

Women filling out the questionnaire who had been date-raped, not necessarily as their first experience, had a variety of feelings. Some felt responsible for getting themselves in unsafe situations, as if it were their fault: "To end up at a guy's house who I had only met that night, drunk, with no way home, was just stupid." Some were worried about their reputation: "I should have yelled out, screamed, fought for my life! But I was worried that he would tell everyone that I was a liar and wanted it." Others retaliated by spreading the story to their girlfriends about the perpetrator, making sure that everyone knew that this guy was an "unsafe" date, like one woman who claimed, "Soon, all of my sorority sisters were calling this guy 'waterbed man' because he had pinned me down on his waterbed, and I had had to fight to get him off and talk him into letting me go. There was no way that he was going to get off scot-free."

A few women lost their virginity in such situations. This white Texan, now in her late twenties, was only eleven years old: "My mother and I had had a huge fight; she gave me the option to live by her constantly changing rules or leave. I had left before—to cool off after one of our many altercations. This time I went to the house where my friends hung out. I needed sympathy and a safe place. I couldn't spend the night there, but two guys I'd never met, but who were friends of my friends, told me I could stay in their house. Their parents were out of town, and I could sleep on the couch. I rode on the handlebars of one of their bikes. I implicitly (and naively) trusted them; I was only eleven.

"We arrived at a huge Spanish mansion, went to the

den, and raided the bar. I had never drank and became quickly buzzed. We wandered through the dark house to a bedroom, sat on the bed, and smoked pot from a bong. I felt foolish, because I couldn't understand why the room was spinning. I lay down on the bed to get my bearings. One of the guys started brushing my hair with his hand and then he kissed me. Rapidly, his hands moved toward my pants. I pushed him away. One of the last conscious things I heard was, 'You can have her. She's no good.' My memories are like a slow strobe-light scene from a bad movie. Clothes torn. One of them holding my legs apart. Screaming, screaming for my mother. Being thrown in the bathroom to vomit.

"Later when I woke up, between the two boys, I got up and walked back to my friend's house. I never told anyone for years. For a long time, I wasn't sure if I was a virgin or not. I remembered pressure. I didn't know if it was fingers or penises or what. I felt betrayed, I didn't call it rape for at least ten years, and I didn't tell my mother. She had never protected me, and I had nightmares for a year filled with shame about sex.

"I don't think I had a normal sex life until I was twenty-five and had an incredibly patient and sensitive partner. We explored each other for five months and then found birth control with which we were both comfortable.

"I'm still healing from the rape. Just in writing this, I question who I was screaming for in that big dark house as a little girl. I think I was calling for the goddess, and I hope those guys are damned to eternal impotence.

"I was only eleven. It was not fair. It was gang rape. I still hate men when they abandon me. I still think they can use power over me in disgusting and degrading ways. I've never been in a healthy, committed, long-term relationship."

Although some stories begged to be concluded or followed up, what some women left out often came across the loudest, like the following story from a white, thirty-two-year-old from Texas. How does she feel now? How has the event affected her sex life? She doesn't say. "I lost my virginity to a boy on the first and only date we ever had. He asked me if I wanted to go parking, which then meant kissing. After we were out in the country, he demanded sex. I said adamantly, 'No!' So he held me down with one hand and his body and ripped my clothes off with the other hand and raped me. I felt dirty and ill afterward. When I got home, I got drunk and didn't think about it for nine years. Now I think about it often."

A similar story comes from a white woman from Ohio, who was raised a Quaker. "I can remember very little before I was raped by my boyfriend. He was older and in college. I visited him and was staying in the girls' dorm with one of his friends. I remember him chasing me across campus in the dark mists, afterward.

"I remember he wrote out a check for a million

dollars to keep me from telling anyone. I left the next morning. I didn't tell anyone. It didn't seem like sex, but sex since then has seemed like that experience: a kind of resignation to the man's sex drive and tremendous confusion on my part. My body felt scorched. I think rape has defined my experience. I cannot turn away from it. I don't believe I know what sex is. What it's for."

This woman, a twenty-two-year-old student from Kansas, feels grateful that penetration did not occur during her "date molestation." But she doesn't reveal what, if any, were the lasting effects of this event: "One of my first sexual experiences occurred when I was sixteen. An older neighborhood boy, whom everyone thought was the greatest, invited me to his house. We were down in his basement when he began kissing me. I was in such awe that this popular boy could like *me*, the mousy kid, that when he began to take off my clothes, I froze. As I stood there naked, he tried to have sex with me by pushing me against a cement wall and awkwardly stabbing at me with his penis. Suddenly I snapped out of my numbness, and realized that I needed to leave. He wouldn't let me go and was holding me so tightly that I eventually had to hit him to free myself. Luckily, he had not been successful in penetrating, only scaring and humiliating me. Later, I discovered that all of the neighborhood boys were watching us through the windows outside, betting if he could make it with the quiet, shy girl. I was devastated and have only told two people this story. I have tried to put it in my past. Luckily, my 'real' first experience was much more positive."

Some women kept their experiences of date rape a secret and shared it here for the first time ever. Feelings of shame, guilt, and self-blame kept them from letting anyone know. Others, like this twenty-six-year-old white woman in sales, told their families or an authority figure without hesitation:

"From a medical standpoint, I lost my virginity when I was twenty. I was in college and was date-raped. The night of my sorority spring formal, I went to the dance with an old family friend. Four years prior, I had gone to my junior prom with this same guy and had had a wonderful time; he had made me feel like a princess. So, when the opportunity arose for me to go with him to my sorority formal, I was really excited.

"At the dance, I got drunk and he asked me if I wouldn't mind going to his mom's house so we could sleep in a bed. At his house, we began touching each other. I took off my dress and he took off my panties after he had taken off all of his clothes. As he entered me, I told him, 'No! No! Stop!' He said, 'Keep it down, my sister is in the other room.' I kept quiet because I didn't want my family to know that I had gone to his house and gotten myself in this situation. Instead, I tried to push him off and turn away. He was stronger and didn't stop

---

In some regions of Italy, it was the custom of a suitor to abduct and deflower a female, then offer to marry her.

until he was ready to ejaculate. He pulled out after he was 'satisfied'and rolled over and went to sleep. I lay there softly crying to myself. I was in a state of shock! We didn't say much when I left.

"When I got home, I immediately told my older brother of the incident and he called the guy's mother. I later told my mother and some of my close friends, who helped me deal with it. When this happened, five years ago, date rape was not discussed as openly as it is now. If it happened today, I would have dealt with it differently. I would have turned him in. I still see him occasionally and think about the incident. We don't talk and I despise him. I can't tell you how cheap it made me feel.

"The one incident I choose to think of as my first time, since it was consensual, happened when I was twenty-three with someone whom I cared a lot about and still do. He was one of my first boyfriends who I had been dating since I was nineteen. When we first started dating, I knew of his reputation as a 'ladies' man.' However, he knew I was a virgin and respected that at first. I understood his need for sex (he was twenty), so I satisfied him with oral sex, which didn't bother me. I do remember that one time I told him I was ready. He put on a condom and then couldn't go through with it because he didn't feel that the time was right for us. We eventually broke up because he wanted a 'guarantee' that we would be in a sexual relationship within a year. I told him I couldn't guarantee that—that in life you couldn't guarantee anything! We continued to keep in contact with each other once he graduated from college, and he eventually invited me to come visit him.

"It was two weeks before my twenty-fourth birthday, and I considered myself a virgin, despite the rape. I felt ready to make love and wanted him to be my first. He had no idea, when I arrived, that I was seeing him with this intention. Initially, it was awkward when I first saw him. We went out to dinner and things began to go better. When we got back to his place, I told him what I wanted. We proceeded to have sex. After he came, he took a shower and I remember thinking how glad I was that I finally had sex and wondered why I made it such a big deal."

An engineer from Ohio in her mid-thirties has just recently learned to call what happened to her date rape: "At age seventeen, I was dating a much older man. He was not a kind man, but he was a man. I was so naive and innocent. My destiny, I believed, was to marry and have kids since I was not smart enough to go to college and become a teacher or a nurse—the only options available to me, or so I thought. Many times he had pressured me to have sex, and I told him no—if he needed sex, go find a prostitute! We became engaged, but it was all a big joke to everyone except me, who thought it was real and took it seriously. I must have put my mother through hell.

"I worked evenings at a Dairy Queen and after work

this guy and I would go park. I didn't know that I could refuse him when he forced me to perform oral sex on him. I didn't know what it was, except that it felt wrong, in the dark and in the car. I got no pleasure out of these experiences; I never even got touched. Anyway, one day we arranged to go to the mall. I got ready. All nice girls wore girdles back then. I drove to his parent's house where he lived. Although it was a pre-arranged date, he was in the shower when I arrived and his parents were gone! He demanded that I come into the bathroom and wash his back. I refused. He demanded I come into the bedroom. Reluctantly, I went. I don't know why, but I undressed when he insisted. I guess I was afraid he wouldn't like me anymore. And all I could think about was how ugly and weird the girdle would look. Without me really knowing what was happening, he was suddenly on top of me. I was so scared. It hurt; then it was over and I felt nothing. I was humiliated, discomforted, depressed, ashamed, and stupid. I got dressed; he got dressed. We went to the mall, first stopping at my poor mom's house to change my underwear, which had gotten bloody.

"Because this first sexual experience was so degrading, I figured that Hey, I'm not a virgin, so I might as well have sex with anybody. I felt like cheap dirt after being deflowered, so why not fuck as much as I wanted and with whomever I wanted, instead of having no choice? I got birth control pills and at one point was keeping track of the number of lovers I had—just like a guy.

Thank God I did not get AIDS or anything else nasty.

"I never considered my first time important, but it did have negative consequences and led me to act promiscuously. Years later, I talked with my husband and he said that now they have a name for what happened to me: date rape.

"Sex is so central to life and yet it seems to be such a taboo subject (except now intercourse is almost equated to death because of AIDS). There is so much to sex— pleasure, well being, sensuality—and yet it is so unexplored, untalked about, and hidden.

"Writing about this has been therapeutic for me. What an awful man he was! What an awful experience. What an awful thing to happen to a young girl. How awful that that young girl was me!"

Here's another woman, a twenty-one-year-old salesperson from Missouri, who also realized in retrospect that what had happened to her was not her fault. "It's hard to confront the issue of my sexuality because it has caused me so much pain. It all happened when I was thirteen. I had just moved to a new neighborhood, and on this particular evening I was walking home from a friend's house when this guy (whom I had met once) started following me. We got to the park that was close to my house and he started kissing me. I admit that I really didn't mind kissing him, but I never wanted to have sex. He wanted to, however, and I could not stop him. It was very frightening; afterward I just ran home.

He really hurt me physically, especially since it was my first time and he was incredibly forceful. But emotionally, the pain hurt even worse, because I held it in for so long and nobody knew what happened to me that night.

"At that time in my life, I hadn't heard of rape or acquaintance rape. My mother had talked about strangers in parking lots and never saying yes if someone wanted to give you a ride. But she didn't warn me about this guy, a friend of my friends! Deep down inside, I was frightened and hurt—this was a nightmare—but on the outside I denied everything. I acted like nothing happened—nobody was to know especially because I was willing to kiss him.

"This experience kept me from any close relationships with males for many years. Because my father was never around, I never had any positive male role models. I didn't really like my body at this time in my life either. I was developing, and it seemed to be in all of the wrong places. Also, at this time having friends and being accepted was very important, and I did not want anything to keep me from having lots of friends.

"It wasn't until I developed a close relationship with a guy in high school that I began to open up and confront the past. We didn't have a sexual relationship, just hugs and closeness and honesty. When I entered college, as a psychology major, I began to learn more about relating to others. I began to open up to new friends and realized that what I had been through at age thirteen was wrong. He should have never gotten away with what he did to me (and what he probably did to other girls as well). In college, I also met a special man with whom I fell in love and finally enjoyed being sexual. I began to love myself and my body and learn that I was a special and unique young lady."

This twenty-five-year-old white Californian does not call her first experience date rape, but her story certainly depicts a lack of consent. She also gives a graphic picture of subsequent sexual acting out that many other women who had been violated also report:

"I had had a history of flirting with a friend's ex-boyfriend, with whom she was still in love. She told me to lay off, so I did and told him to do the same. My friend had a party, which all three of us attended, and we all proceeded to get horribly drunk. I was sixteen, weighed about 120, and did about twenty shots of rum. My next memory is of lying on the floor in the dark, on my back, with this guy rolling over on top of me saying, 'Let's have sex again.' No one was around; we were in the family room. I had two simultaneous thoughts: What does he mean 'again?' and This isn't how it's supposed to be. I pushed him off, but then tried to give him head, feeling utterly confused.

"To this day I have no recollection of the actual experience. I hadn't planned on sleeping with him ever, and was terrified that my friend would never forgive me. I waver between feeling raped and feeling stupid. Everyone tells me I was fully active and talking during the blackout; I remember nothing.

"From this experience and a strange chain of others, rumors spread around school that I was a slut. This definitely led me to act out and I went through a period of excessive sexual activity. I felt that if everyone thought I was a slut, I might as well play the part. I cultivated my sexiness: wore tight jeans, mastered the double entendre, could elicit a whistle. But when the time came for even kissing, I'd shake uncontrollably, thinking the guy would find me out. Needless to say, I was never physically satisfied with any man! Still, I felt a sudden sense of power, twisted power though, since it required erasing myself to achieve it. I could make a man want me and do foolish things simply by allowing him to sleep with me. For a long time I felt that a man would be with me only if I slept with him—quickly, well, and often. I had no self-esteem and didn't believe that any man could be interested in me for anything but sex.

"My sex life has been tremendously impacted by these early years. To this day I find penetration difficult. All the foreplay is wonderful—I love to be stroked, kissed and rubbed, but when it comes time for him to penetrate, I tighten up, literally. Only a very patient man can succeed, and then he has to be prepared for failure occasionally. In the past, I have tended to be attracted to

---

It was the custom of some Romans to require the ritual deflowering of a virgin with the wooden phallus of the fertility god, Mutunus Tutunus, before consummation of her marriage.

young boys, because, as my current boyfriend suggests, I want to give them the wonderful first time that I didn't have. But I always feel sad, because we're not in love. I had my first orgasm with a man this year—all these years later."

Feeling guilty or responsible for what happened can have extreme consequences, as this thirty-two-year-old from Oklahoma relates. "I have thought about my first sexual experience many times in the past thirteen years. Even to this day I don't feel I have resolved it in my mind.

"I first met the young man when I was seventeen. He was new in high school, extremely good-looking, and arrogant. I was pretty naive. He first approached me at a Mexican restaurant where he was working. We went together for about three months. We had some heavy make-out sessions, but I certainly would never sleep with him because of how I was raised. Through him, I found out I was a pretty sensual person, but eventually he dumped me, and I was heartbroken. He was my only serious high school boyfriend.

"About two years later, when I had just finished my freshman year of college, I encountered him again. I was a little wilder by then, but still hadn't slept with anyone. I went to his house. I only intended to visit him and roll around. Well, the entire situation got out of hand; we had always stopped before intercourse, so I figured we'd stop again. He just kept going though. I was dry—

it hurt like hell. He said something like 'I know you wanted it.' Then he left the room. I've never seen him again since that day. I remember clearly getting in my car and just crying on the way home. It wasn't exactly how I had planned on losing my virginity. I went into the bathroom and, of course, there was blood.

"To this day it still makes me unhappy to think about it. I wonder to myself, did I really 'want it'? Was I date-raped? It was not a pleasant experience. For the next six months I was pretty wild sexually. And then all of a sudden I stopped and withdrew into myself. I went from being incredibly wild and overweight to really quiet and thin; I was taken to the infirmary several times because of fainting. I probably lost about fifty pounds around that time.

"As for the boy, I don't hate him, but I do feel angry that I've never had the chance to resolve anything. I've wanted to write about this for a long time. Thanks for asking. Deep down, I think that maybe I did eventually want to sleep with him, but I hadn't planned on it that way. I felt used, violated, just crappy about myself. Right now, I feel a little sad."

One of the consequences of date rape often seems to be a desperate need to rebuild feelings of mutual trust in order to feel safe in future relationships, as shown by this twenty-six-year-old teacher's story: "When I was in my teens, I had some sexual encounters with a few guys, but none included penetration, only kissing and exploring. It was with a guy I knew through my travels with a musical group, who took away my 'virginity' at age sixteen. One Easter vacation when I went to visit him, I had intercourse forced upon me for the first time. I was sleeping in the bedroom next to his. As I was about to fall asleep my first night there, he came in and told me to follow him. I trusted him because he was a close friend of a member of the band I belonged to. He lead me to his bedroom where he proceeded to rape me. He told me it was supposed to feel good, even though I kept telling him it hurt. He stuck a number of different objects into me and told me that these were things I could do when I was lonely for him. I remember the blood and thinking how much it hurt.

"There was one man in my life with whom I convinced myself that I had found my forever love. Our relationship grew out of a friendship of a few years. We lived together for two years and loved each other very intensely. Though we never had sexual intercourse, we had physical contact in just about every other way. I was still healing the wounds of my past, the rape, and he understood. I truly thought that nothing could be better than this. But I left him after two years because I knew I desired sex with women more than anything else. I thought in leaving him I could step toward my true desire, but I wouldn't acknowledge this to myself because I didn't feel supported by myself or anyone else. So I went back to the security of his arms just a few months later. We knew each other so well, and I thought no one could ever love me the way he did—and that I would never feel so comfortable with anyone else.

"Last year I ended our relationship as lovers for good when I moved to San Francisco. I was able to do it because I knew I was in a safe place that would support my true feelings. He was my best friend and I have lost him completely. He will not talk to me and I miss him terribly. But I had to be true to myself and follow my own path, not the one prescribed by society or the one that I felt I 'should' follow."

This forty-seven-year-old counselor from California married the man who forced himself on her. Hers is ultimately a tale of hope and the possibility of healing. "He was my high school sweetheart of two and a half years. It was his last night before leaving for college in another state. I had said no to intercourse for the whole time we'd been together. We were in the car, and I said no in the heat of passion; but this time he pushed himself into me. I had the vague knowledge that 'it' had happened. When I got into the house, I saw the blood, and sat by the front window crying 'til dawn (my parents were on a rare out-of-town trip). I felt sad, abandoned because he was leaving, angry and resentful, since I figured he would be screwing girls at college. I also felt ashamed. Once I joined him at college two years later, I got pregnant immediately and was horrified. A college-town family physician took pity on me and induced a miscarriage.

"We married after college graduation. During the entire marriage I was never turned on and had a lot of buried resentment. Later, through years of counseling and sexual experiences with other partners, I came to love my sexuality and indulge with my partner freely. Psychoanalysis set me free as a whole being. I left analysis and my marriage at age twenty-seven, feeling great about myself, attractive, and attracted to men in healthy ways."

By breaking the code of silence, women who have been wounded by abuse can hopefully begin to heal. And as we as a society are finally able to speak about sexual violation, perhaps we can begin to educate ourselves, our daughters, and sons, to shape a future where these negative experiences are nonexistent.

Women Loving Women

"Because two women together are incapable of the central act [copulation], their existence as lovers has been denied, downgraded to harmless play, or viewed as a perverted obsession . . . Lack of anatomical knowledge or absorption of phallocentric norms may account for some of the female, as well as male, bewilderment over lesbian lovemaking."

—*Martha Barron Barrett,*
Invisible Lives

Even more than for heterosexual women, there is a glaring lack of information and research on sexual initiation of lesbian women. Of course there are many books on coming out, lesbian erotica, and recovery from sexual abuse. But nowhere could I find statistics on how many lesbians had sex with men first, or at all, were sexually abused or raped, or, having been exclusively with women, have their own definition of "virginity loss."

I experienced a variety of reactions when I spoke with lesbians about the concept of virginity. Some had their own personal definition which they used to fit their lives—they didn't take society's meaning too seriously. As one lesbian shared in her questionnaire, "What exactly constitutes losing 'lesbian virginity' is a debate among many lesbians I have talked with. For me, it is a matter of having oral sex in which both participants give pleasure to each other."

Others were offended by the very notion. They felt that technically, according to society, they were still virgins, although they were complete sexual beings.

They were irritated that penile/vaginal penetration and hymenal rupture was the standard for marking the beginning of sexuality.

Most of the women who tell their stories here are those who consider their "loss of virginity" to be their first sexual experience with a woman. A few women who first had sex with men but later turned toward women are also included because they consider the latter to be the more significant event.

One of the women who responded unambivalently about her first time with a woman being her "loss of virginity" was this forty-nine-year-old psychologist from Arizona: "My loss of virginity was very mutually desired, with a young woman with whom I had recently fallen totally in love at age fourteen. We were very ardent, passionate, from kissing to full nakedness and kissing and touching all over, to genital touching. I was ready and it felt wonderful and powerful. I also felt extremely guilty, however; I was a very pious Catholic at an all girls Catholic high school who wanted to be a nun. This didn't fit, but I didn't care. I felt alive in a new way—like together we had created this marvelous, new, previously undiscovered thing. We were surprised at what we had done but glad to have discovered it.

"After my first encounter of 'going all the way' in lesbian terms, I felt guilty when I thought about how the Church and my parents would judge me, but not guilty in the act of lovemaking. I did feel set apart from my friends; I started a secret life with no one but my lover to talk to. I felt deviant, but proud of the new power. Later, after experiencing some strong condemnation, I felt dirty and sinful, but still happy in moments of passion.

"I once tried to fall in love with a boy, but he remained just a friend. I looked up meaning of *homosexual* and was very scared, but didn't talk to anyone about it. A later turning point was when another woman told me that she loved me *because* I was a woman, that there were many women who loved women. That was the moment I entered the lesbian community—at least mentally— and felt less isolated, more real, as if I didn't have to be grateful for someone allowing me to love them."

This white, retail grocery buyer from Georgia, born twenty-five years later, was much more comfortable identifying herself as a lesbian at a young age: "I had known from early on that I was a lesbian. I did choose to wait to have sex, wanting to have my first encounter to be with a woman and not a man. When I finally found someone, at age eighteen, the situation was rather stressed. The woman I got involved with was my first gay friend's lover. So the betrayal of a friend led to my first lesbian relationship.

"Despite this, once we made love a tremendous weight was lifted from my whole being. I felt I'd finally come home from being lost. My mind was reeling with the sensation that a woman was letting me touch her and enjoying it.

"Once I started to be sexually active, I never wanted to go back to a sexless life. I always find myself watching sex, whether in magazines, TV, or movies, heterosexual or homosexual. I'm very much a voyeur; that's where I think I learned about sex, what to do and how to do it. I was and still am insatiable in the beginning, middle, and end of my relationships. I'm very passionate about the women I get involved with; showing someone how I love her through sex is an important part of my being. Being sexual can be too demanding on those who haven't really, can't, or won't come to grips with their own sexuality and aren't comfortable enough to just let go two to three times a day."

A thirty-five-year-old graphic designer from Wisconsin also knew she was a lesbian at a young age, but didn't meet the right woman until much later. "One of my first memories is of her naked body against mine and how wonderful it felt to kiss a woman. I'd had boyfriends and always hated the whisker-burn feeling after heavy kissing. Kissing a man felt wrong to me, though, and nothing much more ever happened between me and men. I'd known since twelve that I was a lesbian, so when, at age twenty-five, I finally fell in love, I was so happy."

Other women came to lesbianism much later. A fiftyish white Californian tells her story. "Technically, my 'first time' was with the man I married. But I never physically enjoyed sex with him in twenty years of marriage. Sometimes my heart was engaged, but my body never was. I just went through the motions. Consequently, my husband told me there was 'something wrong with me.' He blamed all of the foreplay we had done before marriage, saying it was psychologically damaging without intercourse. He made me feel like it was unhealthy to just arouse each other without going all the way.

"Unfortunately, for twenty years my view of sex was defined by my experiences with my husband and his opinions about my lack of interest, my inhibitedness, and my inability to fantasize and try new things. Over the years I suppressed so much rage, it never felt safe to be open about my feelings. Looking back, it's no wonder I was also so out of touch, literally, with my body. As a child I was taught not to touch my 'bottom,' and even in the shower always used a washcloth as a buffer between my hand and myself. My mother used to point out other children who touched themselves as naughty.

"When I was finally ready to learn about my female body and strength, I was inspired to call an old friend, my first love from high school—who happened to be a woman. During nine months of counseling and two weeks of intimacy, I awakened the fire in me. It felt so safe being with a woman and easy to talk about our bodies and feelings. Finally, at age forty, I felt like I had come into my own body, in my own hands."

Several women who define themselves as primarily heterosexual also report lesbian "first times." "Prior to [intercourse with a man], I had a sexual experience with a woman," writes a twenty-eight-year-old white Texan. "I was fifteen, and a close friend of mine was friends with an older girl who was a lesbian. Because this woman seemed so normal and was natural and unguarded about her sexuality, the idea must have been planted in our heads. One night, my friend and I experimented, and I must say it was satisfying, although we never tried it again. We are still close friends and speak openly about the experience, for which I am grateful. It could have become an embarrassing wall between us, but instead we chose to just accept it and think of it as having a positive impact on our friendship."

Most of the more sexually explicit stories I received were from lesbians. One possible reason is that because of social stigmatization, lesbians are forced to define themselves primarily by and through their sexuality. Through constant reminders that they do not fit the nuclear-family prototype and that they are not accepted by mainstream society, the lesbian women who answered the questionnaires were compelled to make peace with themselves and seemed more willing to reveal themselves—at least when given the chance to do so anonymously. This twenty-nine-year-old manager from Wisconsin offers a good example:

"I was twenty-one and had never been sexually

involved with anyone. I wasn't particularly interested in men and was too naive to know that I was interested in women. I became friends with two women who were rumored to be lesbians, and one of them began to pursue me. Over the course of many months, I grew brave enough to let myself feel sexual when I was around her, and I knew that eventually I would make love with her. Of course, all of this was set against a backdrop of fear, anxiety, guilt, and confusion. These emotions, combined with a sense of breaking a taboo, made me feel like a raw nerve ending. When she invited me to her house one night, we both knew it was inevitable.

"The year was 1973 and I sat on a bar stool with my head down on the bar in the basement of her home. She was five years older and had been with women most of

---

"For a long time, we have had no representation of absolute femininity, that is, one defined neither by relationship to lover, nor to a child, nor with a father, nor to a husband.

"In fact, femininity is rarely represented in the absolute, but rather in relation to some other reality of the masculine world. Usually, when a woman withdraws into a territory closed to the male, she is perceived as a pariah, a sorceress, or a crazy woman. When depicted in literature, cinema, or television, feminine virginity occurs generally in a tale about a male introducing himself into this realm and transforming the virgin into a 'real woman,' as if femininity could never be complete in itself."

—Ginette Paris, "Pagan Meditations"

her adult life. My body was on fire and I could not speak. She sat next to me—always patient and gentle—stroking my hair on the back of my neck. I could not lift my head from the bar, for I knew she would kiss me and that thought singed the hair on my head. Finally, after at least an hour of her soft breath on my neck and gentle coaxing, I lifted my head and she kissed me. My internal organs rearranged themselves, my heart rate doubled, I could no longer breathe, and I felt my legs melt into a puddle underneath the bar stool.

"We kissed for hours, and when my lips began to hurt she took my hand and guided me over to the couch where I collapsed in anticipation of what was to follow. She began to touch my breasts, stomach, and thighs. I felt a most incredibly passionate panic in my body, as though someone was dancing on my chest and I couldn't catch my breath. She removed my shirt and brassiere, now touching my skin directly. The panic became more excruciatingly exquisite as I began to understand where her hand would go next. When she finally put her fingers gently but very deeply into my vagina, the dancers on my chest tried to kill me! But somehow, miraculously, I survived and lived to experience many thousands of dance marathons since then. It took years for me to work through the guilt I had about being a lesbian, but from that moment on I knew with utter certainty that there was no other path for me.

"In the first year after I came out, I struggled with my new identity, where I would fit in, what friends and family would think. But my concerns were never about the actual experience of sex with a woman. No, indeed! The sexual experiences I had and continue to have with women felt to me like a coming home to myself. From the very first kiss, I knew in my body that I had arrived at the part of myself that was true. I became very aware of my body, and with the help of many loving women along the way I came to love and appreciate my physical self. I felt beautiful and attractive to other women— something I never felt with men. I felt empowered, utterly independent, and capable in the world and in my interpersonal relationships."

One issue that comes clear through the questionnaires is how many lesbians in this small sample reported a history of childhood sexual abuse or rape. Some women stated explicitly that such experiences had made them choose to be with women, because they didn't feel safe with men. As Martha Barron Barrett wrote in *Invisible Lives: The Truth About Millions of Women-Loving Women,* "Incest might indeed have an impact on the sexual orientation of survivors. It just isn't what you've been taught. It may make boys wonder if they are gay; it may make girls wish they were." Indeed, several women who had been raped or abused reported lesbian experiences to be very sexually healing, which led them to decide to be with women.

A twenty-nine-year-old "recovering Catholic" park ranger from New York is typical of this position. "My first time was not a good experience, although the relationship lasted another eight months. He became very possessive and pressured me to make a commitment; he even used the *M* word and talked about children. I wanted nothing of either, certainly not at the ripe old age of seventeen.

"Shortly after this, I was raped by a 'nice' boy who took me to the junior prom. But even before I had my first consensual sex, I was molested by two brothers who baby-sat me when I was five to six years old. I wasn't able to admit this or tell anyone until I was twenty-one. This corresponded with my first relationship with a woman. I don't think this was a coincidence. A tremendous amount of rage had been building up inside of me, including anger directed at my mother because I had tried to tell her about the rape. The lack of resolution of these experiences made me extremely angry with men in general.

"With the woman I loved, I finally felt secure enough to confront these occurrences. It was such a positive experience, healing in so many ways. I really consider this my first time because there were no outside influences, no pressure. She was as nervous as I was—it was my first time with a woman and her first time with anyone. What was nice was that there were no patterns or models to follow; it was so unknown, with no distorted images from commercials or movies to be a certain way, to act or perform a certain way. It was a very sweet and innocent experience. I felt like I was participating 100 percent and felt completely equal. There was no gender communication gap. It was wonderful to be with someone who was unique and different but understanding and familiar at the same time.

"This was probably the most positive and significant sexual experience I've ever had. It was healing and set a positive path for future relationships with both men and women. It was a turning point from past negative patterns of low self-esteem, the feeling of no control, no equality, and little pleasure. Coming out for me was very easy because it was such a relief to understand all the muddled messages that hadn't made sense before. I felt very free. Unfortunately, because I was open and extremely straight-looking, my coming out was threatening to my straight friends. I lost some good friends because of their homophobia.

"I have since had a relationship with a man that's been satisfying and healing; I'm not afraid of men anymore. Although my preference remains primarily toward women, I feel good that it's no longer a reaction to my fear, anger, feeling of helplessness, and an attempt to escape men."

Two of the women who had a history of childhood sexual abuse and came out in later life report of becoming pregnant the first time they had sex. "My 'first' sexual experience was with the man I was engaged to," writes a forty-nine-year-old white psychotherapist from Massachusetts. "Two weeks before the wedding we couldn't wait any longer. We had been engaged for two years, had heavily petted, holding off for the 'proper' time. I should have been more concerned about using a 'proper' birth control method, because nine months later, I was a mother.

"I remember very little of the physical sensations. In part, this may be due to my family history, which I've recently uncovered. In the past few years, in therapy, I have remembered incest; my father was sexually inappropriate, and my grandfather and mother were perpetrators in our family, my brother and I the victims. This has left a huge scar on my heart. Sometimes I just wish for peace and rest. Safety is an enormous issue for me, as is sensitivity to invasion and boundary violations.

"When I was thirty, I fell in love with a woman. She loved me and I opened to her a sexual side of myself I hadn't known existed. I have discovered with my lover an essence of loving and being sexual that transcends the limits of earlier sexual experiences. She has offered to me in her loving, a presence, a holding, and an expansion I cherish. This loving gently nudges me to risk beyond where I thought I could go before. It has been an initiation unto my self."

A black thirty-nine-year-old child-care specialist reveals a parallel experience. "Early childhood incest has deeply colored my sexuality. It involved an older family member when I was between the ages of seven and fourteen. I can't remember the exact details and I really don't wish to talk about it. Let me just say that I have spent years and years learning how to heal and emerge from my sexual repression.

"The actual 'loss of my virginity' was probably slightly typical for the era. I spent a year and a half dating him before we seriously talked about having sex. Finally, I felt ready—like I had reached womanhood—and decided that it was time. Unfortunately, I became pregnant the first time, and we had no other recourse but to marry. Neither of us believed in abortion at the time. This thinking has changed for me, thank God. During my marriage, sex wasn't a priority in my life. I felt guilty about my body and, after a certain point in my marriage, about sex in general.

"One divorce later and the remembering of my incest experiences, I now realize that I was incredibly repressed where my feelings about sex were involved. Not until I had my first lesbian relationship did I feel satisfied physically, emotionally, and spiritually. It was the best coming out story in my life."

Whether there is actually a relationship between incest and lesbianism is a matter of much debate. In *Secret Survivors: Uncovering Incest and its Aftereffects in Women*, E. Sue Blume states emphatically: "The fundamental inaccuracy of the argument is that one is not gay by default, that is, who one loves is not defined by who one hates. A woman who hates men because she was molested by a man does not gain the capacity to be aroused by women. One may, indeed, hate the very gender that one is attracted to." And psychiatrist Judith Herman reports, also in *Secret Survivors*, that her research "does not support the presumed connection between incest and homosexuality; the overwhelming vast majority of incest survivors remained steadfastly, even doggedly, heterosexual."

Notes Blume, "Although incest does not create homosexuality, it does indeed have an effect on lesbians. In addition to possible self-doubt, self-hate, and confusion, the lesbian incest survivor re-experiences many themes of the incest. The lesbian lifestyle involves stigma and, for some, shame. It can elicit guilt over what one's sexual feelings or experiences are. By living in the closet (all but the most courageous and fortunate lesbians need to pass as heterosexual at least sometimes), the lesbian incest survivor adds yet another secret to her sexual life."

Ultimately, as the stories shared here reveal, whether a girl knows from childhood that she loves women, or an adult woman comes out after twenty years of marriage and three children, whether she is an incest survivor or comes from a run-of-the-mill family, each woman has her own truth, her own experience. As Martha Barron Barrett comments in *Invisible Lives*, "Women-loving women are everywhere, and their lives are as varied as those of women whose erotic attention is focused on men. As a Washington statewoman said, 'The only thing true about all lesbians is they are all women.'"

The Romantic Minority

"I was delighted by how many varied responses I got when I asked people to define good sex. Some people said good sex had to do with communication. Others said it had to do with connection. One man called it a physical statement of self. A woman called it a body language and a mind game that reveals the face of the soul. It's not one thing."

—Julia Hutton,
discussing her book, *Good Sex,*
in *The Oakland Tribune,* August 26, 1992

Each of the stories in this section comes as close to an ideal first sexual intercourse experience as would seem possible in this culture. The women here somehow transcended conflicting stereotypes to embrace their sexuality as a natural and wonderful part of themselves to be explored and cherished. Gabriel Garcia Marquez eloquently writes of such an encounter in *Love in the Time of Cholera:* "Then it was she who took the initiative, and gave herself without fear, without regret, with the joy of an adventure on the high seas, and with no traces of bloody ceremony except for the rose of honor on the sheet."

Although circumstances differ, there seem to be several common ingredients: conscious choice, emotional connection, and physical awareness and readiness. These women felt free from outside pressures—they consciously chose to have sex without their partner's urgencies or parental or religious guilt looming over them. They also felt love, an obvious element but probably the most difficult to find. When they were touched emotionally, they could then feel comfortable with physical intimacy.

Communication was also crucial. It often helped to raise a young woman's self-confidence level and brought about connection, enabling the woman (and probably the man, too) to feel more comfortable and cared for. What easier way to alleviate awkwardness and fears than to discuss feelings beforehand?

They also chose partners who were physically sensitive and emotionally caring. Unlike women in other chapters, these women shared the fact that they were virgins and therefore allowed their partners to be more physically sensitive. As a consequence, these women were most often enveloped in feeling of emotional safety by their loving partners, which helped bring them into their sexual being.

Lastly, they realized that making love is a powerful vehicle for connection, even the first time, but they didn't have unrealistic physical expectations. Although the experiences related here are all incredibly positive, there are only two instances when young women had an orgasm the first time. But those who didn't have orgasms also didn't place pressure on themselves or feel unfulfilled. They knew that it was just the beginning.

This twenty-eight-year-old auditor from Texas typifies a person who had all of the right elements: "Although I was raised a strict Southern Baptist and was taught that I should wait until marriage, I felt that the time was perfect when I chose to lose my virginity, despite the fact that it was supposedly 'wrong.'

"When I was seventeen, I had been dating a boy for some time who was sweet, understanding, and gentle; I never felt any pressure to have sex with him, which was probably why I felt so good about my decision.

"One night we were at a party with friends, and after everyone left we started intense, passionate kissing. He was very slow and tender, softly telling me he would be very careful and asking me questions. After the initial attempt, we bathed and then tried again—this time more successfully. I could not have asked for a better partner. We dated for a while afterward and now are still friends. If not for him, my first time would never have been so wonderful and gentle."

To most women, the emotional satisfaction seemed to be much more important than physical fulfillment the first time, and loving words were much more important than physical dexterity. This forty-year-old Jewish psychotherapist from New York relates her experience: "I was going out with the boy of my dreams. I was eighteen, in my second semester of college, living away from home for the first time. We had discussed making love before it happened, and I told him that I was a virgin. He told me of a past relationship that marked his first sexual encounter; I would be the second girl he would make love to.

"I was nervous, excited, very much in love, and ready. We went to his dorm room. Chances are good that we had a beer or smoked pot, since that was a fairly regular occurrence. So we may have been comfortably altered by drugs, but definitely not drunk or wasted. I remember making love on a mattress on the floor, extremely happy to be sharing such a significant, personal event with him. Although I felt comfortable and in love, and my partner was conscientious, it wasn't especially pleasurable the first time. I think we were both so excited about doing it that not a lot of time was spent in foreplay and therefore his entry was somewhat difficult. Our sexual relationship improved greatly after that, and we fully enjoyed each other sexually, socially, and emotionally.

"One thing that has always stood out about that first time was that there was no blood. I remember searching the sheets looking for the telltale bloodstain but the sheets were clean! I've always wondered why: Did my hymen break from horseback riding, wearing tampons, or had I perhaps been sexually abused sometime in the past and just blocked it? I don't know the answer, but I was disappointed, because I had expected to see proof."

"Making love is a form of worship for your incarnation. It is a way of acknowledging with and through the presence of another person that we have come here in a form that longs to physically engage with one another. In making love we are attracted, we are drawn to, we are fulfilled. We are overjoyed by one another, time and time again."
—*Daphne Rose Kingma, "A Garland of Love"*

Here's a forty-year-old white Catholic woman raised in Massachussets who presents another ideal story: no parental voices, religious dictates, social pressures involved, simply the natural, intuitive, trusting process of love taking over. "I was sixteen when I met Matthew (twenty-two) at a summer camp, where I was a lifeguard and he was a counselor visiting from England. We fell in love and every evening stood on the front porch of my cabin talking, hugging and kissing. Even though curfew was at 11:00 p.m. and the camp was run by Christian fundamentalists, somehow we were considered the darlings of the camp and were allowed to stay up until all hours, which we did, all night, every night, for ten weeks. When summer was over we pledged undying love, and Matthew went back to England, promising to return the following summer. Romantic letters flew across the ocean all year; finally summer returned and so did Matt.

"Although the previous summer had just been hours of passionate kissing, when he came back we very quickly progressed from standing on the porch to sneaking off into my room. We never discussed having sex and certainly not birth control. He claimed to be a virgin also, but even at the time I couldn't believe a twenty-three-year-old man in 1970 could possibly be. In retrospect, I'm sure he was lying—my lack of pain, his finesse, all point to prior experience.

"Apparently, trans-atlantic passion had been building. One thing just led to another in a haze of lust and romance one night in my room. I felt that it was just right—that I loved this man and was ready. Afterward, I really felt wonderful; I truly believed that in that act I had become a woman.

"I think we had sex several times before my hymen actually broke; I don't remember pain or very much blood. I didn't have an orgasm then—or for many times thereafter—but I felt loved, fulfilled as a woman, and, frankly, proud that my sexuality had had the chance to emerge in such circumstances—no guilt, no sense of loss.

"It was the perfect hallmark for my sexual awakening. From my first experience onward, I have always valued the spiritual aspects of the experience, with whomever I am with. Sex that leads me to the holy—that's what I strive for."

The transcendent possibilities of sex, alluded to in the preceding story, are eloquently elucidated by Daphne Rose Kingma in her book, *A Garland of Love:* "Making love is more than physical self-indulgence, more than physical relief. It is the dialogue between two souls, the interface of the material and spiritual." This twenty-eight-year-old skin care specialist from California describes another story of closeness and spiritual connection: "It still makes me cry at the beauty of it . . . he was so tender, slow, and gentle. He even made me wait until I turned eighteen, because I was under age. This waiting was painful for both of us. Shortly after my eighteenth birthday, we began making love. Managing to achieve penetration was difficult; my body was tight and it hurt a lot, but I told him to stay with it. I was overjoyed to no longer be a frightened virgin! Neither of us climaxed, but that wasn't necessarily the goal. There was a spiritual specialness we both felt, which was both moving and magical."

Rarely did women actually have an orgasm their first time, even under perfect conditions. This sixty-year-old white writer raised in Illinois was one of the few. "We knew it was going to happen, and he'd bought condoms. For four years on and off, I'd been dating a fellow student—a class ahead of me, son of a professor—at a small, church-affiliated college. I was twenty-one. We were comfortable enough with each other, but we had always stopped just painfully short of intercourse until after I'd graduated. We were sober—and ready. The coupling, after some juicy foreplay, took place in his mother's car, in a farmer's field near my hometown, which was ten miles from our college campus. The rubber held. My orgasm was a whole body experience, and I felt great. Who thought about disease in 1954?

"Two footnotes to this event come to mind. First of all, only weeks later, I learned that my partner had had a homosexual experience. He brushed off the incident by saying that he had not initiated it. Secondly, the night after my first time, I again had intercourse, this time with a different man, a close friend of long standing. He had, until then, had only homosexual liaisons since age twelve. Thank heavens AIDS hadn't yet entered the picture."

Sometimes, the most unbridled passion that women felt in their lives was during puberty, when their actions and thoughts were uncensored by adulthood responsibilities and worries. A fifty-two-year-old teacher from Ohio tells her tale. "My sexual initiation was the standard kind of the '50s—parking and making out. I was as eager a participant as my high school boyfriend and certainly felt I was ready in every way but, of course, I was naive and inexperienced; we were fifteen. We didn't need drugs or alcohol. Our pure, untamed hormones rushing through our bodies were quite enough stimulation.

"I still remember those evenings; they were probably the most intense emotional and physical feelings of my life. The orgasms were incredible even without penetration. Thirty-five-plus years later, I can still feel the sensation of his lips. He was an unsurpassed kisser.

"But hard as it is to believe in this day and age, penetration never occurred. We honestly believed you couldn't get pregnant without it. What a shocking surprise to us when the worst happened.

"Though we continued to date through our freshman year in college, the resultant problem and our ages led to difficulties. We married others, but I never forgot him or how he made me feel. Twenty-five years later, at our class reunion, I'd come alone and he was widowed. Though nothing physical happened, every intense feeling resurfaced. We kept in touch and a year later spent an entire weekend together. Two years later, I had the courage and strength to divorce my husband of twenty-eight years after his repeated refusal to seek help for his alcoholism. By this time, my first love had remarried. We appear to be star-crossed lovers.

"No one has ever aroused me in the same physical and emotional way. My only experiences are with this man and my former husband."

Some women wisely chose to be with sensitive, supportive men who could help them overcome previous bad experiences. "Growing up," writes a thirty-five-year-old Pennsylvanian, "boyfriends had mauled me—I never had sex with them, but it was a literal fight not to. I was very developed at an early age, and men and boys would comment and, in many instances, grab at me or even attack me. I was the girl who was always trapped in the back seat on the school bus as free game. Fortunately, I always somehow got out of these situations physically unscathed—but I was emotionally bruised.

"I developed a hatred for and fear of men that I have to this day. I find that I'm attracted to what my mother calls 'soft' men. Over the years I've also had relationships with gay men, because there was no threat of their wanting anything more from the relationship other than intellectual and verbal stimulation.

"Despite these negatives, my first sexual experience at age nineteen, with the man whom I eventually married, was wonderful. We went to a hotel for a weekend, because a friend was being married in another state; this somehow made it okay for our parents. We were completely in love, and I felt fine afterward. What affected me the most was that we had had plenty of previous opportunities to have sex, but Joe had insisted, 'No—I want the first time to be special.' And it was.

"I'm thankful that I found Joe because he gave me a safe place to confront many issues revolving around sexuality. After much therapy, I have resolved my aversion to the typical man who views women as his property for sex and catering services. I have also come to grips with the damage that the Catholic Church has done to women. This happened when I was sending my own daughter to Catholic school, and she begged me to get her 'out of this place.' She complained that the nuns were beginning to tell her that what she was feeling— sexual curiosity—was amoral and wrong. I listened and put her into another school without a strict religious curriculum. Through her I learned that I could not continue the cycle of having women demoralized for their sex. No way would I subject my daughter, who I wanted to raise with high self-esteem, confidence, and self-respect, to the convoluted ideals of the Church."

Certain women's partners helped them accept their bodies and feel beautiful. As one young women explained, "When I was sixteen, I had a very critical boyfriend who was always pinching my butt and exclaiming how flabby it was. Then I fell in love with someone who thought I was the sexiest thing alive— and suddenly, I realized I was!"

Body image seemed to improve with a partner's sensitivity and adoration, but sometimes outside help came into the picture, as another woman relates. "When I was sixteen or seventeen, I read in a popular women's magazine (amidst pictures of stunning models, ironically) that being sexy was a state of mind: If you truly believed you were sexy, so would your partner. Since I was—like most teenage girls—modest and insecure about my body, I knew that only a change of attitude could help me feel better about myself. Amazingly, this fashion magazine inspired me with a message that had a tremendous impact on my life and forever changed my self-image."

A white twenty-two-year-old student from Illinois exemplifies the process of overcoming insecurities with the help of a caring partner. "The first time my boyfriend and I tried to have sex, my mother walked in on us. Talk about upsetting! After that we agreed to wait, and then, three months later, we uneventfully had sex. He was patient and understanding, and I was typically uncomfortable and a bit scared.

"At first, I was very modest and insecure about my body, but my boyfriend kept telling me that it was perfect the way it was, and that even if I weighed twice as much he would still love me. Amazingly, a transformation took place and I began to like my body, which I had been ashamed of up until then.

"In this respect, my first experience was very positive. I also changed my belief that sex should be reserved only for marriage. I don't believe in sex for immediate gratification, but think it is invaluable as a learning experience between two people who truly care about and love each other. And love is not exclusively a marital arrangement!"

Here is another story from a twenty-two-year-old from Kansas who had a similar experience with a loving partner: "When I was in high school, I felt that I was ugly and didn't belong, probably a familiar feeling for most hormone-harassed teens. Senior year things finally began to change; I was tired of feeling bad and began to focus on becoming the person I wanted to be. This vote of confidence in myself indirectly led to a very select internship opportunity the summer before college. It was my first time away from home, and I ended up meeting a wonderful guy who was twenty-seven. We dated the entire summer, becoming close friends, and a week before I moved back home, he suggested a weekend away from the other interns.

"He was the perfect gentleman. A walk on the beach,

dinner, dancing, and then we topped the night off with a glass of wine. After our incredibly romantic evening, he asked me if I wanted to make love, and I was stunned! (He knew I was a virgin from previous discussions we had had.) I instinctively felt that this was the right time: He was the right person, I felt comfortable, trusted him, and it was the perfect environment. He went slowly, explaining and checking in as he went, showing me how wonderful making love was. If I wanted to stop at any time, if I felt nervous or it hurt, which it didn't, he wanted to know, he said. Afterward, I felt blissfully happy and comfortable; it had been like the romantic scene in the movies that never happens in reality, a softly lit, slow motion, tender entwinement of love. This wonderful, caring man showed me that I was a special person. Thankfully, I had this positive experience after my other, humiliating one."

For some women, time was important in helping them feel comfortable. This thirty-three-year-old housewife from Massachusetts reports, "I had been enjoying a non-physical relationship with a man for over a year. Gradually our friendship blossomed as we enjoyed outdoor activities together: camping, hiking, tennis, etc. When the time came to be intimate, it was the first sexual exploration for each of us, even though I was already twenty-two. We were very slow, gentle, and sensitive of each others bodies and needs, touching and exploring carefully, enjoying each sensation.

"When he entered me for the first time, it was an amazing feeling—my body was certainly ready! I was afraid and excited at the same time. Because I felt so safe and comfortable, it was a beautiful experience, which grew into more fun and playfulness and touching and love throughout our four-year relationship. I felt very blessed to be with someone who was also new to learning about sex and was willing to listen to my needs and feelings. My partner was ten years older than I—a male virgin at thirty-two! It was a learning experience, understanding how my body worked and the mysteries of being a woman; it was wonderful and stimulating.

"I had always been tuned in to my body and my emotions, so my emerging sexuality was a continuation of new sensations being awakened inside of me. My dad wanted me to feel guilty, but I didn't; I felt sure of myself and happy in my relationship. I had some real independence and a sense of power and control over my life. I was proud of my sexuality and am to this day."

A twenty-one-year-old student from Nebraska chooses to think of her second time as her first time. "I was very wrapped up in my friends and sports and not emotionally ready for sex in high school. But when I finally was ready, it felt like I gained an important part of my life.

"My first experience was with a boyfriend in college. We had intercourse one time; there was drinking involved and it was extremely uncomfortable. In fact, we didn't try it again, even though we continued to date for several months.

"My second experience was very special to me; it was a turning point in my sexuality. We had dated for over three months and waited until I was comfortable and ready. It felt like my true first experience, as making love. He concentrated on making me feel good and eased slowly and naturally throughout the evening. I couldn't care less about 'losing' my virginity; what matters is the growth potential of making love to the man I love. I do believe that intercourse is an important part of consummating a marriage and miraculously making babies, but it's also an incredible way to show that you love someone. Losing one's virginity is important, because you must be mature enough to face the consequences and emotionally ready to communicate with your partner. Choosing to make love and lose my virginity was the right step for me."

Sometimes, women defied the odds their circumstances and training would seem to have dictated and had fantastic, romantic first times, as this forty-three-year-old psychologist raised in New York tells. For her, everything came together just right. "Though we lived in upstate New York, which was somewhat liberal, our family of five daughters was subjected to the same double standard of expected behavior that was common everywhere prior to the 'sexual revolution.' My mother seemed to feel that girls who were brought up properly didn't get into the 'wrong' kind of situation with boys; my father felt that any red-blooded American male worth his salt would 'go after it' whenever and wherever he got the chance, and it was the woman's responsibility to make sure things didn't go too far. All of these ideas were communicated through guilt and innuendo. It was all very insidious.

"The only thing I remember my parents stating specifically was the fact that men had a strong sex drive and women didn't. They certainly must not have realized the effect this piece of misinformation would have on me. When I felt the pangs of first love and burgeoning sexuality at fourteen, I denied the reality of these feelings. After all, a woman's sex drive didn't exist, did it? This cutting off of feelings was completely passive and vulnerable to whatever atrocities anyone wanted to perpetrate on me. Fortunately, most of the boys I dated didn't take advantage of my passivity and were usually discouraged by my lack of response, concluding that I was either not interested in them or that I was frigid.

"I remember sitting around with the other girls in my dorm in my freshman year of college in 1968 comparing notes on the extent of our sexual experiences. Out of twenty-five or thirty eighteen-year-old women, not one admitted to having lost her virginity. We were students at William & Mary in Virginia, an exceedingly tradition-bound bastion of conservatism where a high premium was placed on a coed's reputation. A very small number of bohemian types openly flouted the prevailing mores, but they risked expulsion from school for doing so.

"Ironically, within two years, specifically relating to campus-wide political strikes in the wake of the invasion of Cambodia and the killing of student protestors by the National Guard at Kent State and Jackson State, the entire climate at my school changed. Huge numbers of students began to openly defy administration policies relating to dorm visitation and the right to demonstrate on campus. Opposition to the war in Vietnam seemed to clear the way for changes in attitudes about civil rights, black power, feminism, sex, and drugs. It was a time of great questioning, challenge, and experimentation. Most of these changes were inspired by idealism. Even experimentation with drugs was seen as a means of consciousness expansion, unlike today where drugs seemed to be primarily a vice for coping with emotional pain.

"So amid this clash of changing and conflicting ideals, I met Greg. His preparedness for any and all of life's eventualities made him an exceptionally safe first partner. (By contrast, two of my closest friends in college became pregnant during their very first sexual encounter.) Greg and I had a number of wild, drunken evenings together, where we stopped short of actually 'doing it.'

Shunammitism was an ancient religion that worshipped the healing powers of the scent and breath of the young virgins of Shnam.

"There was much more to our affair, however, than hormones, obliterated consciousness, and groping. Greg and I had a profound intellectual connection and believed we were passionately in love. He in particular wanted to make everything perfect and right for me—and for us—for my first time. He borrowed a car, booked a fancy hotel room in Washington, D.C., and set the scene with candles and romantic music. We made ourselves a picnic of French bread, wine, and cheese. The entire event was planned in advance with richly savored anticipation.

"Greg was also prepared with birth control. He had a supply of condoms, contraceptive foam, and K-Y jelly. Beyond that, he had a savings account set aside for an abortion and airfare outside the United States if all else failed. This was good.

"Although Greg was responsible for all of the forethought and planning, I concerned myself with the inner psychological process of trying to determine with certainty that I was ready for this stage of physical and emotional adulthood. Fortunately, the previous summer, while talking about sex, a trusted male confidant admitted to me in a moment of candor that any man who claimed to cherish virginity in his fiancee but was not a virgin himself simply had an ego problem of excessive territoriality. What a brilliant revelation!

"Thus, the sexual initiation I had with Greg was a moment, unlike so many others in my past, for which I was fully ready—physically, emotionally, intellectually, and spiritually. He was patient and gentle with me. It was an overwhelming sensation of total merger, but not beyond my capacity to contain and integrate. I realized that even though I had had more intensely erotic experiences, I had never felt this vulnerable, open, and receptive. It was clear that an experience of this magnitude would have been too overpowering emotionally had it been thrust upon me at an earlier age. I felt grateful and in love."

As all of these experiences reflect, the discovery of sexual intimacy can be exquisite. Choosing the right partner and the appropriate moment when you feel ready, discussing fears and feelings with your partner beforehand, and educating yourself with proper information and self-knowledge can pull young women out of the "getting-it-over-with" position to a place where they can look forward to their first sexual encounter with anticipation and excitement.

Losing
"Losing Your Virginity"

"The word 'virgin' did not originally mean a woman whose vagina was untouched by any penis, but a free woman, one not betrothed, not married, not bound to, not possessed by any man. It meant a female who is sexually and hence socially her own person. In any universe of patriarchy, there are no virgins in this sense."

—*Marilyn Frye*,
Willful Virgin: Essays in Feminism

Asking the question, "How do you feel about the term 'losing your virginity'?" provoked many strong viewpoints. The majority of the women who answered believed that the term had negative implications but disagreed widely about what those connotations were. Women pondered the metaphoric associations, felt that the term itself pressured girls into sex, and questioned why the term was mainly applied to women, to name a few typical reactions.

Taken as a whole, their responses reflected the entire spectrum of feelings that our society has about female sexuality—from resentment toward archaic double standards to believing that the phrase is accurate because a prized commodity had been lost. Following are a sampling of the responses:

"It's kind of silly, really, because innocence in our culture is lost at such a young age. I lost my virginity, in a way, when I was eight and realized my mother was not the mother I wanted and my father couldn't be trusted. I lost the sense of safety that is so important to children at a very young age. It has been a long struggle since. In that sense, there's almost no such thing as a virgin in our culture over the age of ten."

"A slang term that shouldn't be used. It makes young girls feel pressured into having sex before they're ready. There's too much hype involved."

"I don't like the term. Somehow it conjures up visions of losing some great treasure. Why don't we treasure our initiation into sexual intercourse with another? Though this 'loss' is indeed painful and awful if it is due to rape or sexual abuse of some sort, often we gain access to lovely possibilities of joining with another human being."

"I like it. It's quaint. It is a turning point for a woman with no going back. I believe she should hang on to it until 'Mr. Right' comes along."

"It seems to put women in a helpless role. It wasn't 'lost,' because in effect we decided to give it away. What would be a better term? Who knows!"

"I remember back in high school, even junior high, it was so important to guys to be with a girl who loses her virginity. In my crowd of friends, it was "in" to be vocal about losing your virginity and with whom. But I kept my experience between my boyfriend and myself while everyone else slept around."

"I can't think of any other term to use as a substitute, but I don't like it at all. If one's first sexual act was always positive, maybe we could say something like 'setting your spirit free.' I like that much better, but it doesn't always fit."

"It's a negative term. I think it puts a lot of pressure on young girls, and older ones too. It makes it sound as though all of the pressure of sex is put on the female. It is as though if she has sex, she has lost a part of herself, whereas it should be a very special time for a girl. It also makes it sound like boys have nothing to lose. It is as though this is a goal that they are striving to achieve. This is not true for all people."

"The term implies that you turn into a different person after intercourse, which in most cases is not true. It also implies that you're no longer whole, which also isn't true."

"I think it's somewhat harsh. It gives the impression that something has been taken which can never be returned. In a way this is true. On the other hand, I think it discourages girls who may have had sex but now want to abstain. They might think it doesn't really matter now, that it is too late. Also, the idea that something is lost rather than gained connotes negativity. It makes girls and women feel bad about losing their virginity instead of feeling wonderful about experiencing their sexuality in full for the first time."

"It is not something that I lost. It was my decision to have sex. *Virgin* is a term that most women don't like to be labeled with because it has negative connotations. I felt that way. I felt less of a woman sometimes around my friends who had had sex. Now that I have matured a little, I have more of an attitude that I don't care what others think of me; it's just what I think of me that matters. I didn't lose my virginity, it just changed."

"I think it's inadequate in its description. All in all, I felt like I had lost my virginity long before the actual act."

"I didn't lose anything. I gained more knowledge about myself as a physical, emotional, spiritual, and sexual being. Words are just words. Terms are just terms. It's not the letters, it's the intent. Each person's experiences are just right for her. We are all perfect beings."

"I feel it has very negative connotations. Instead of gaining a beautiful experience, it implies we lose something. And we lose it to men. It's just another way of considering women as men's property, rather than as equals."

"I personally am not offended by the term, although I know it upsets many other women. I didn't feel I 'lost' anything, except my hymen, which I was glad to have done."

"I wish it didn't have the negative connotations it does in our society. I was always very self-conscious about being a virgin until I was twenty-three. It just never felt right, and I was uncomfortable with it, but more uncomfortable with compromising my principles. I think sex is way overrated through the media—let alone inaccurate. 'Losing your virginity' is made into something much more than what it is. Maybe we should look more at the *emotional* with the physical, rather than just the physical."

"I felt I lost some power when I lost my virginity because it was the only thing I had of my own that I hadn't shared until that point."

"It's an anachronism from feudal times, when a woman was an item was to be owned and possessed. I hate the term."

"I didn't lose anything, but rather gained knowledge. I didn't lose virginity, but became a sexual being. My only real regret is that I wasn't a little older. I might have spared myself a few silly sexual encounters. Maturity usually brings restraint; I could have used a little restraint a little sooner."

"It seems sort of archaic. I would never use the term in conversation. Seems pretty sexist, but I'm not rabid about it. 'First experiences of intercourse' seems much more straightforward and non-sexist to me."

"Wouldn't it be wonderful for young women to think of being sexually healthy as letting their bodies and emotions respond when ready? It would have been so much easier to have not felt the pressure to 'lose my virginity' and join the gang at school who were all having sex (of which, it turned out, there were several lying virgins and several lesbians having intercourse to ward off coming out)."

"It seems like a joke to me. Sorry."

Dear Abby:

I have a problem that is probably unlike any you have ever received. I am a twenty-six-year-old woman who is about to be married. I have never had sex, but when I was 24 years old, I agreed to be artificially inseminated and gave birth to a child for a couple who wanted one, but the woman was not able to have a child.

Now here is my question: Am I still a virgin? My husband-to-be is well aware that I want to wait until our wedding night to make love, so he has never pressured me. I need to know if I am still a virgin.

Yes or No

"Because the experience was painful for me, I really do not like the term. I would rather talk about who was my first true love or the first time I enjoyed having a sexual relationship. Sometimes I wonder if 'when, where, and with whom' you lost your virginity is important at all. If this time is special for some people, I'm happy for them and would gladly like to listen to their story of that experience, but for me, I want to talk about the special friendships and relationships I've had, not the one night I lost my virginity."

"A person's first sexual encounter should be something special with someone special, and a man and woman should be sexually active only when they are emotionally ready. But society places a lot of emphasis on 'losing your virginity' and builds it up to a big deal that leads to a lot of people being let down and disappointed. I don't feel I look any differently since I lost my virginity. I don't know if it's because I waited so long or not."

"I did lose mine, in spite of fighting hard. I didn't get the chance to share the first time with someone special.

Dear Yes or No:
  Since you have never had sexual intercourse, you are still a virgin.
  If your fiance is not aware that you have given birth to a child, I suggest that you tell him.

So for me, 'losing' is accurate."

"I do not like the term at all. There is so much more to sex than just intercourse. I think if more emphasis was put on other aspects of sexuality, maybe people would take things more slowly. Other things can be just as satisfying, if not more so, than intercourse."

"It's a stupid term, only associated with experience of traditional intercourse. In some people's minds it is okay to fondle, perform oral sex, and do other activities so long as you stay a 'virgin.' How ridiculous."

"It had a mysterious meaning for me before—as with all girls in my neighborhood. When it happened, I didn't bleed, didn't have pain. Nothing that I had been warned about happened! The term created negative connotations and also communicates control of the female."

"It's a terrible phrase. I learned that losing your virginity before marriage is bad, being a slut, and dirty. But what if you have anal intercourse, oral intercourse, or anything else sexual, are you still a virgin? I think it puts ridiculous pressure on people. Boys are pressured into losing theirs and girls are pressured into keeping theirs until they are married. I think kids need to be taught differently about sex or they will have bad experiences like I and many others have had."

"This term is so unfair. Men are studs if they lose theirs early and take as many females with them as possible. Women, on the other hand, are sluts if we sleep with many men."

"I don't think we're prepared to know what it means. It can mean everything and nothing. It's a term overburdened with purchase, ownership, and passivity; it needs to be unwound to discover its meaning. Maybe it means, 'they didn't get you yet, but they will. Be careful.'"

"Too much emphasis is put on the event. Being a virgin is not necessary to being a good person, especially for women, and men should stop trying to play conqueror. It's sick."

"It's stupid. As if it's something to be valued. It's a very male way to look at a woman—as if he owns her and her sexuality."

"The term is ridiculous, patriarchal, and meant to serve as a way of controlling sexuality—especially women's. Women who are virgins bring a high price at market. Men who are virgins are laughed at."

"I feel I lost my virginity the first time I performed oral sex on my boyfriend at age seventeen. The other type of 'virginity' is too easy to take away from a female.

Oral sex was me consenting, knowing what it was, performing it out of love. It was mine to give away."

"This is such an old-fashioned term and sounds so holy, like women are something not to be touched— those you screw and those you marry. I object to the term *virgin*. Losing usually implies a negativity, however losing one's virginity should imply the discovering of sexuality, pleasure, and spirituality. The finding and defining of a new dimension of self."

"I don't think that this term carries the same meaning and impact as it did in my youth. Whereas it used to be reprehensible, today it seems to be the main objective of girls as well as boys."

"For me, it's probably an accurate term. I was too young and didn't have the self-esteem or maturity to share completely in the experience--I was passive, so in a way it was lost."

"I agree with Shug in *The Color Purple:* If you haven't enjoyed it, it isn't sex and you are still a virgin. I thought for a while that technically you have to have been penetrated by a penis, but when my sexual-abuse recollection came up my view changed. I've also been reading a little about goddesses and the perspective of sex as a sacred kind of initiation. It turns current cultural ideas on their heads. You are even more sacred and powerful after sex. For me, I will no longer be a virgin when I've been fully present and involved and satisfied in sex; when there is no longer a part of me watching, cringing, being terrified."

In the past, the term "losing your virginity" had some logic to it, though it was based on a faulty premise. After all, since the worthiness of an unmarried woman was measured according to her sexual purity, and her subsequent marital status was the measure of her value, her virginity *was* a commodity "worth" something—the trade off to get the "right" husband.

Now, thankfully, women have a larger barometer by which to measure their worth and identity. Because our scope has widened, the term "losing your virginity" no longer accurately reflects our present reality. As so many of the women who responded to the survey note, our sexuality is *ours*; it is never lost, never given away to another, it always belongs to us. The inception of sexual relations is the beginning of new experience gained, our sensuality now shared.

What We Can Learn From These Shared Stories

Afterword
by Louanne Cole, Ph.D.

There can be many sexual "first times" in a
woman's life:
- her first sensations of arousal toward another
  person
- her first kiss,
- her first time "petting" or "feeling up" (depending on your generation)
- her first orgasm,
- her first one with a partner,
(and, the subject of this book,)
- her first intercourse.

Yet, for generations women have knowingly assumed that intercourse was the unstated subject of the
question, "What was it like for you the first time?"

Why does intercourse fascinate us so? One reason is
that intercourse can lead to pregnancy—the creation of
a life—and in some instances can lead to life's virtual or
actual destruction. It may also have this premium position because it intimately couples two body parts that
are seldom seen in public. It is one of the very few ways

in which physical boundaries are merged and, as the Moody Blues song says, "two wrestle as one"—with a part of one literally inside part of another. Its potential as an imprinting experience of intensity and shared passion registers with most people, whether gay, bisexual or straight.

The women in this book have answered the question about their "first time" with as wide a range of stories as is imaginable. As readers, both female and male, you have had the opportunity to chat intimately with them as though they were 150 best friends disclosing their personal odysseys. Some were tales of confusion, discomfort and regret. Others are filled with task-oriented resoluteness or with ambivalence. Still others were romantic, sensual, emotionally and sexually fulfilling steps toward intimacy and womanhood.

A Romantic Springboard

Which stories you remember most will depend to some extent on your own experience and how you have framed that memory (or what you anticipate if you haven't yet had your own "first time"). I encourage you to make use of the valuable opportunity here. Focus on what worked for the "Romantic Minority." Use the information these women shared as a springboard for your own sexual enjoyment, or bring it to your friend, mate, son, or daughter.

If you have had regrets about your own first time, know that you can grow from that original starting point. Recall the many stories of women who stated that even though their first intercourse was less than ideal, they believed it could be better. And, true enough, many found that their sexual experiences got better as they themselves grew and became more comfortable with asking for what they wanted.

Our society oscillates between awe-filled fascination with intercourse and phobic avoidance of its impact. Because we as a culture have not yet made our peace with sexuality, we resort to ostrich-like head-in-the-ground medical and legal policies, yet eagerly tune in the latest "shriek-of-the-week" TV talk shows. We want to know the dirty laundry, but we don't want to deal with it.

Our experiences as women crossing this symbolic threshold reflect our culture's discomfort with sexuality. Ours is a body-phobic culture. We have believed and sometimes falsely taught our children, particularly our female children, that it is dangerous to let our bodies feel "too" good. The theory presupposes that hedonism will overrun our positive goals, cause societal decay, and leave us all devoid of virtue.

So, it isn't surprising that approximately 15% of American adult females have not yet experienced orgasm by any means of stimulation. In many ways, the "Romantic Minority" have defied the cultural odds by swimming upstream against the forces that would negate female sexual pleasure. These forces have created the fallacy that there are only two choices: the "good" woman and the whore.

Fostering Exuberant and Responsible Sexuality

This dichotomy between the "good" woman and the whore reflects our hesitancy as a culture to endorse female sexuality, much less reward it. A movie such as "Ramblin' Rose" stands virtually alone as an example of art where a sexually exuberant, likeable young woman is understood and accepted by her adopted family, protected by them from a "complete" hysterectomy at the hands of the local physician who believed it would desexualize her.

We owe it to our sons and daughters to teach them the language of sexual communication and sexual self-esteem that is not wrapped in the terms of fear, pain, or threat of death by AIDS. Yes, they need the facts to make safe decisions, but they need more than that to join the ranks of "The Romantic Minority." Otherwise, at best, they are simply rolling the dice while we look on, hoping they "luck out."

Our daughters need to feel okay about asking their partner for what they want sexually and not censor themselves for fear of coming across as "too demanding" or "too experienced." Too many young women have tolerated painful intercourse because they were afraid of "hurting his ego" rather than expecting him to say, "How wonderful to know exactly what you want!"

How Specifically Can We Pass a Better Legacy on to Our Daughters?

First, we need to openly share information about how to make good sexual decisions. This involves stating what some of the obstacles to a good experience might be:

- misuse of alcohol and other drugs,
- being in an unsafe location,
- being with someone you barely know,
- hurrying,
- doing it only because he really wants to, or
- lack of effective birth control and protection against sexually transmitted disease.

This also involve stating what conditions are likely to enhance a first experience:

- a sensitive, informed partner who is known to you and willing to talk about your feelings,
- a safe, well-timed location,
- adequate birth control and protection against sexually transmitted disease, and
- the right time in your own emotional development.

A good experience is also made more likely when a stable foundation is laid by earlier life experiences. Female children should be permitted, if not encouraged, to masturbate and go through an age-appropriate private and personal sexual self-discovery. A young woman who knows her own body can more effectively describe her desires to her partner. Even Kinsey found in the 1950s that women who masturbated to orgasm before marriage were more likely to be orgasmic with their husbands!

Bodily self-acceptance also stabilizes a young woman's sexual foundation. This includes teaching accurate names (the external female genitals are called the vulva, not the vagina) and comparable parts for the genitals (the female clitoris is the comparable part for the male penis, not the vagina).

Instruction, whether at home or in class, should emphasize that a wide range of body parts variation is "normal" and attractive. I have counselled far too many adult women who didn't know the location of their clitoris (the primary site of sexual stimulation for most women). Others have suffered from the "cloaca syndrome," thinking that all their excretions and menstrual blood passed through only one body opening "down there."

Young women also need to understand that there is no formula for how sex is supposed to happen. Unfortunately, when little or no information is available, too many women resort to soap opera or romance novel sexual depictions. Depending on what she looks at, a woman can have unrealistic expectations of earthshaking rapture (much like winning Wimbledon when you've never picked up a tennis racquet) or extreme fears of pain which, when taken to their furthest extreme, can result in a bodily expression of that fear called vaginismus (a clamping down of the vaginal muscles).

Sex for Secondary Reasons—A Common Error

Girls also need to understand that sexual expression is like other types of personal expression. Its variation in intensity and enjoyability is dependent upon many ingredients. In the case of sexuality, a key ingredient for an enjoyable "first time" is mutual, not unilateral, interest in creating pleasure for and with one another. Regrettably, too many young (and older) people engage in sex for secondary reasons—and young women are the most likely to do so.

One of the most sexually destructive messages that has been sent to young women is the false notion that their sexuality is a commodity and should be treated as such. Most people have heard some form of the expression, "Why would a man buy the cow if he could get the milk for free?" where the woman is the cow and sexual access is the milk.

Economic principles have been applied by both men and women to women's sexual experiences, and especially to intercourse. In the interest of "protecting" women from making unwise sexual decisions, many words have been uttered:

"Don't give it away too easily"
"Did he at least take you to a nice restaurant before you went to bed with him?"

"You slept with him too soon, you'll never hear from him again."

And some men have done their part to maintain the commodity line of thinking as well:

"So, did you get any?"
"I really scored Saturday"
"Did she put out last night?"

We wince at these phrases and we know their negative effects, but the ideas behind them are far from gone. And this is despite the shift in the popular common wisdom from: "Save it until marriage" to "You can do it, but only if you're in love" to "Do it so you won't be a virgin anymore."

"Doing it" to shed the stigma of being a virgin is another way in which young women have sex for secondary reasons. "Doing it" only to be accepted by one's peer group is driven by the same group pressure that we associate with young men in urban gangs forced into an initiation rite to prove their manhood.

"Doing it" only to assure oneself a steady boyfriend or a date to the prom are also secondary reasons. "Doing it" only as a political statement or one of rebellion to parents are other examples. These reasons omit the primary aspect of human sexual expression: the conscious, intentional sharing of pleasure.

Fulfilling Sex without Intercourse

Basic sex education should also include the idea that individuals can have very fulfilling sexual experiences without intercourse. What we have called "foreplay"— hands, mouths, genitals, and hips pressing—can be equally, if not more, stimulating than intercourse for women. The simple act of allowing intercourse in no way leads directly to sexual sensitivity or competence as a partner.

Before the age of easy access to birth control, many men and women who wanted sexual experiences with one another (without risking pregnancy) learned to create wonderful levels of pleasure without intercourse. Too many young women have learned by experience that "going all the way" didn't necessarily lead to their going all the way to orgasm without preliminary or simultaneous direct clitoral stimulation. Shere Hite found this so for about 70 percent of her respondents.

"No" Means "No"

We also need to educate our teens about the fallacy of believing that "no" means "maybe" and "maybe" means "yes." Sexuality should always involve consensuality. If one person is no longer experiencing pleasure, the other should pause and ask why, and ask what can be done about it—no matter how far into the sexual experience.

Until this becomes the common wisdom, we will also need to describe date rape. Learning to have an appropriate level of caution while dating requires a delicate balance between alertness and trust of men. Lack of information produces an unsafe level of naivete; tales of horror can generate antisocial levels of paranoia.

No one can pick out a date rapist at twenty paces. They are, however, often not good at listening to others' requests and sometimes exhibit a sense of entitlement that goes way beyond a healthy level of self esteem. (No such accusations can nor should be made toward "bad listeners" with large egos because date rapists are only a minute subset of that group.) They easily see others as things for their personal exploitative sexual use. And often they were taught that sex is really not at its best unless there's a coercive element to it.

The Power of Vicarious Experience

It is my hope that as you read this book you had the opportunity to rethink and, if needed, to reframe your own "first time." If you have not had intercourse, I deeply hope you will reread the stories of "The Romantic Minority" and take in their attitudes and how they made their decisions. Incorporate as much as you can to enhance your chances of having a similarly enjoyable experience.

Male readers, you've gotten a wonderful and rare experience of listening in on emotional descriptions of one of life's potentially most intimate moments. You have certainly learned that no one thing makes all women tick and that no one sexual technique satisfies all women. Yet one theme emerges throughout these stories: most women desire open, easy going, sensitive communication as part of their "first time."

I expect many women who read this book will have experienced some kind of emotional release. I did. This was a rare experience, and a privilege. Although as a sex therapist I've heard life stories of hundreds of clients for ten years, I've never had the opportunity to explore this primal topic so thoroughly.

The voices in this book often resonated with me. I felt a special comraderie with these women. At times, I said to myself, "I could have said that." The last time I felt this kind of resonance led to my selection of my life's work in the field of sexuality—as an educator, writer, and therapist. That experience was my reading *The Hite Report* in 1977, the first study of sexuality in the language of women. It didn't just tabulate and analyze, it opened an emotional window. So does *The First Time*.

Because *The First Time* lets every reader vicariously experience a wide range of "first times," I hope it will inspire many heartfelt, empathic, and informed discussion between potential lovers, parents and children, and friends.

Bibliography

Martha Barron Barrett. *Invisible Lives: The Truth About Millions of Women-Loving Women.* New York: Harper & Row, 1990.

E. Sue Blume. *Secret Survivors: Uncovering Incest and Its Aftereffects in Women.* New York: Ballantine Books, 1990.

Susan Brownmiller. *Against Our Will: Men, Women and Rape.* New York: Bantam Books, 1975.

Frederique Delacoste and Priscilla Alexander, eds. *Sex Work: Writings by Women in the Sex Industry.* Pennsylvania: Cleis Press, 1987.

Alice Echols. *Daring to be Bad: Radical Feminism in America 1967-1975.* Minneapolis: University of Minnesota Press, 1989.

Sigmund Freud. *Sigmund Freud: Volume XI.* London: Hogarth Press, 1910.

Betty Friedan. *The Feminine Mystique.* New York: Dell, 1963.

Marilyn Frye. *Willful Virgin: Essays in Feminism.* California: Crossing Press, 1992.

Susan Griffin. *A Chorus of Stones: The Private Life of War.* New York: Doubleday, 1992.

Shere Hite. *The Hite Report: A Nationwide Study of Female Sexuality.* New York: Dell, 1976.

Julia Hutton. *Good Sex: Real Stories by Real People.* Pennsylvania: Cleis Press, 1992.

Molly Ivins, *Molly Ivins Can't Say that Can She?* New York: Random House, 1991.

Samuel S. Janus, Ph.D. and Cynthia L. Janus, M.D. *The Janus Report on Sexual Behavior* New York: John Wiley & Sons, 1993.

Karen Johnson, M.D. *Trusting Ourselves: The Complete Guide to Emotional Well-Being for Women.* New York: Atlantic Monthly Press, 1991.

Daphne Rose Kingma. *A Garland of Love.* California: Conari Press, 1992.

Kinsey, et al. *Sexual Behavior in the Human Female.* New York: Pocket Books, 1965.

Marty Klein, *Ask Me Anything.* New York: Simon & Schuster, 1992.

Niels H. Lauersen, M.D., Ph.D., and Eileen Stukane. *You're in Charge: A Teenage Girl's Guide to Sex and Her Body.* New York: Fawcett Columbine, 1993.

Catharine A. MacKinnon. "Does Sexuality have a History?" *Michigan Quarterly Review,* v30, n11, June 13, 1993.

Rosalind Miles. *A Woman's History of the World.* New York: Harper & Row, 1988.

Anne Moir and David Jessel. *Brain Sex: The Real Difference Between Men and Women.* New York: Carol Publishing Group, 1991.

Kathy Peiss and Cristina Simmons, eds. *Passion & Power: Sexuality in History.* Philadelphia: Temple University Press, 1989.

Lillian Rubin. *Erotic Wars: What Happened to the Sexual Revolution?* New York: Harper Perennial, 1990

Joanne Stroud and Gail Thomas, Eds. *Images of the Untouched: Virginity in Psyche, Mythe and Community.* Texas: Spring Publications, 1982.

Alice Walker. *Possessing the Secret of Joy.* New York: Harcourt Brace Jovanovich, 1992.

Daniel Evan Weiss. *The Great Divide: How Females & Males Really Differ.* New York: Poseidon Press, 1991.

Leslee Welch. *The Complete Book of Sexual Trivia.* New York: Citadel Press, 1992.

Naomi Wolf. *The Beauty Myth: How Images of Beauty Are Used Against Women.* New York: Anchor, 1991.

Jennifer Barker Woolger and Roger J. Woolger. *The Goddess Within: A Guide to the Eternal Myths that Shape Women's Lives.* New York: Fawcett Columbine, 1987.

Appendix

Female Sexuality Questionnaire

I am working on a book which will focus on a specific and long-ignored aspect of female sexuality—sexual initiation, particularly the loss of virginity. It is not a scientific or analytical study. Rather, it will be a presentation of stories, your stories. Only you can say what you feel and know—which is why your words and those of the many other women I'm contacting are the most important part of this book. This is your opportunity to tell about real-life experiences you have lived through. Whether painful or touching, these experiences are worth telling. Hopefully, it will bring us closer to understanding ourselves.

The idea evolved because I noticed that there were very few books on beginning sexual experiences of women. Studies exist, but little is done on the emotional experience—the circumstances, the significance. I am working with Conari Press, a publishing company in Northern California whose specialty is books for women. I aspire to write a book that will be sensitive to women's experiences and beneficial to both women and men.

This questionnaire contains four essay-type questions. Following each question are sample questions which are included merely to stimulate your thinking. I really want to hear your own words, so don't feel restricted by the sample questions. I encourage you to write as much as you feel comfortable sharing. If you have problems expressing yourself in writing and would rather tape-record your answers, please feel free to do so. A personal interview with me is also another possibility.

Your name and identity will be held in complete confidentiality.

Because we are trying to survey a wide range of women, please answer the questions below, which will help us represent as many women as possible:

Age
Ethnicity
Occupation
City/state you currently live in
City/state you were raised in
What religion (if any)
Age you lost your virginity

1. Describe the experience of your own sexual initiation. For most people this means losing your virginity. Include as many details as you feel comfortable giving. Some things that you might want to consider are:

was it planned or spontaneous?
did you feel pressured or compromised?

was it someone you knew well, a stranger, a friend?
were you physically ready--how did you body feel?
were drugs or alcohol involved?
were you worried about birth control or disease?
how did you feel afterward, emotionally and physically?
was it with a man or a woman?

2. Did you have any earlier sexual experiences which are also significant to you? Some examples follow:
neighborhood curiosities fulfilled
watching or reading something sexual
voluntary or involuntary experimentation with friends or relatives
knowing that someone was doing something wrong but not knowing why
witnessing something
feeling guilty about participation in some event

3. How did your first encounter affect your emerging sexuality; what kind of impact did it have on you? Some things to think about are:
did you become more sexually inhibited, modest, or reticent?
did you feel disappointment/embarrassment about your body?
was your body reveling in new sensations; was it awakened?
did you feel guilty or humiliated?

did you feel a sense of independence, power?
was your view of sex redefined after this experience?
did it foreshadow future sexual relations?

4. If you have another experience which you think of as a turning point in your sexuality, please describe the experience:
first intimate love
first experience of being physically satisfied
relationship with a woman
rape
incest
coming out

5. How do you feel about the term *losing your virginity?*